A new w

While Edie still tries to make a life for herself, sudden tragedy strikes without warning: so earth-shattering that it changes everything and everyone in her world.

Taking stock of her life, Edie realizes that fate has left nothing—and no one—for her in New York City. It's time to make a new start someplace else.

When she overhears talk about a far-off paradise where an American can live an inexpensive yet still luxurious life, Edie knows that *this* is the next best step for the hapless, hopeless Carow women.

Determined to make the best of their collective lives—and perhaps remake herself into the artist she often dreamed of becoming—Edie sets out to cross the Atlantic and leave behind all things Roosevelt.

Will Edie make a brand new life? Or will destiny come calling, yet again, with an even stranger set of circumstances than before?

WORLD
WITHOUT END,
AMEN

EDIE IN LOVE
BOOK 3

JANE SUSANN MACCARTER

Publishing Services provided by Paper
Raven Books
Printed in the United States of America
First Printing, 2021

Jane Susann MacCarter
World Without End, Amen
Edie in Love Series
Book Three

Hardcover ISBN= 978-1-7368789-4-1
Paperback ISBN= 978-1-7368789-5-8

Subjects: Edith Kermit Carow, Theodore
Roosevelt II, Alice Hathaway Lee, United States
First Lady, 26th President of United States,
Gilded Age, Victorian romance, 1880s politics,
coming-of-age

To my dear son, Kent Edward MacCarter,
also my cheerleader and steadfast publisher of
deserving poets.

How well I remember—dear God, do I ever remember!—how dark my days grew after Papa's death. There was nothing to be done about it, just more resignation on my part, more endurance, and more pasting-on of placid smiles so that no one sees my pain—something impoverished gentlewomen know all too well.

Because of a quirk of destiny, my one chance for new happiness—as a featured dancer at Mrs. Vanderbilt's lavish Ball of the Century— passed me by in the blink of an eye.

One day, I was "in"—then suddenly, I was "out." I never even saw it coming, or leaving.

What are those words again from the New Testament? Something about "Whoever has 'not,' even his Nothing shall be taken away." (Or, in my case, her Nothing is taken away...)

Yes, my Nothing is now well and truly "away" ... trampled, lifeless, and kicked to the corner. What's even the point of going on?

What's it all for?

FRIDAY

23 MARCH 1883

Papa is being buried today. On Good Friday—so fitting.

The gloomy weather matches our sense of loss, hollowness, and inevitable change.

Of the many qualities that may be attributed to Charles Carow in this earthly life—marked by misfortune, falling short, becoming weak, or helplessly shallow—let it also be said that, in many small ways, he was an angel.

At least to *me*.

SUNDAY

25 MARCH 1883

It's Easter Sunday today.

I can only imagine the hurricane of activity rampaging through the home of Willie and Alva Vanderbilt today. Tomorrow night is the Ball of the Century.

I must buy *all* of the newspapers the next morning—not just the staid old *Times*—to learn all about it.

I must—

Enough.

VERY LATE MONDAY NIGHT

26 MARCH 1883

Tonight is the momentous Ball of the Century.

I'm still awake and watching the clock, imagining what's happening moment by moment.

It's 10 p.m. Carriages will line the driveway to deposit gaily dressed guests at the Vanderbilt's front door. Mobs of gawkers will press in on all sides. The police will hold them back.

Miss Alva will be there in the grand reception room, receiving her twelve hundred guests—she couldn't *possibly* press that many hands in greeting, could she?

On the dot of half past eleven, I know that the Hobby-Horse Quadrille group begins to "gallopade" (as Miss Alva likes to say) up and down the grand staircase in complex dance steps.

After the Hobby-Horse group comes the fairy-tale creatures from Mother Goose and then the Opera Bouffe ... after which it's time for ... the Star.

We of the Star Quadrille ... but I am not part of a "we" any longer.

That gloating understudy, Susan Hartley—wearing *my* fantastical, impossibly beautiful costume with the tiny, electric light glowing on her forehead—will captivate the crowds with her fellow dancers as they dip, sway, and sashay.

After the Dresden and Go-As-You-Please sets, the dancers will part in a shower of shimmering, tinsel stars ... stepping back to reveal Miss Alva herself, who will announce in a voice that carries beautifully across the enormous room, "I now pronounce the Ball of the Century *open* ... to all dancers!"

I won't sleep at all tonight.

LATER:
I didn't sleep, at all.

I want to read about it in the papers before they're all sold out.

TUESDAY

27 MARCH 1883

Shortly after dawn today (around 6:45 a.m.)—still wide awake from the night before—I leave the house quietly. Mamma and Em are still snoring away as I head out to purchase the early papers.

First, instead of heading for a newsstand, somehow I "find myself" (I'm ashamed to say) walking along Fifth Avenue inexorably toward Miss Alva's house. Just to … to…

Just to still be part of it, somehow.

I'm glad I do because the streets are literally streaming with fantastical characters from another world. Costumed party-goers are still spilling out of the imposing front doors of the Vanderbilt mansion.

That's right … I remember now Miss Alva's schedule. The party was scheduled to conclude promptly at 6 a.m. after a farewell Virginia reel.

Hundreds of inebriated party guests now stumble about in the early light of day, waiting for carriages with liveried servants to pick them up or calling out for one of the scores of hansom cabs parked along the road. Yes, the police are still very much in evidence—everywhere—to "keep the peace."

Many children (beginning their morning walks to school), together with troops of newspaper reporters (following up on last night's big story), mingle with and smile at the noisy, laughing guests.

I watch for a while, but then it starts making me feel queasy. I leave in search of the morning papers.

Back at home, only Cook and the housemaid are up, so I'm left to myself at the dining room table. A comforting cup of English breakfast tea is safely encircled by my right hand; heaps of newspapers are splayed out before me on the table.

With perverse pleasure and gnawing pain, I start to read the coverage—page, after page, after page—about the Ball of the Century. I don't want to miss even one tiny nugget of news.

"Crowds of onlookers, restrained with difficulty by scores of policemen, pressed forward to catch glimpses of debutantes and members of New York society, attired in their fancy dress costumes, as they were escorted into the mansion."

The papers say that many party guests came dressed as Louis XVI—safety in numbers, I guess. Also glimpsed were King Lear ("but one in his right mind, hopefully"), Joan of Arc, Daniel Boone, Queen Elizabeth I, and even Father Knickerbocker.

Society's Arbiter Ward McAllister was also there, resplendent in purple velvet and scarlet silk (it didn't say who his character was), while Mrs. Chauncey Depew was a vision in "sea-green satin with clusters of silk water lilies" (not sure who she represented, either).

Hundreds of other guests came as pirates, princesses, peacocks, eagles, medieval peasants, and menacing highwaymen … and two ladies even came as "creatures"—one a hornet and the other a cat. (Apparently. the latter even sewed stuffed cat heads onto her dress—ugh.)

While Miss Alva looked queenly as a "bejeweled Venetian Renaissance princess," her very own sister-in-law, Alice Claypoole Gwynn, upstaged Miss Alva—and *everybody* else—by showing up as "The Electric Light." (What *is* it about Alices anyway? Always managing to be the most breathtaking woman in a room.) Alice Gwynn's stunning gown, made of white satin and trimmed with diamonds and small electric light bulbs, was devised around several of hidden "battery" devices; she literally "lit up the room" as only an electric light bulb can.

Of course, electricity is all the rage now, so I'm not surprised someone capitalized on the idea, especially when a couple of New York streets are already illuminated by this marvel— with many more to come. Thomas Edison's generating station on Pearl Street actively seeks more business.

I read on, and on:

"Twelve hundred gaily costumed figures danced and drank amid the flower-filled house, including the third-floor gymnasium that was converted into a forest filled with palm trees and draped with bougainvillea and orchids. Dinner was served at 2 a.m. by the chefs of Delmonico's, working together with the Vanderbilt's platoons of servants. The dancing continued until the sun was rising. Diamonds and other jewels glinted in the changing light. Mrs. Vanderbilt led her guests in one final Virginia reel, and, with that, the ball was over."

I see that the *Times* even printed the names of all the quadrille dancers—they have to, of course, because we are no "mere dancers per se," but each of us a member of New York society (to varying degrees) in our own right. Yes … here I am, listed on page three: "Miss Edith Kermit Carow," one of the Star Quadrille dancers.

This will make Miss Understudy Hartley simply furious. But of course the name lists of everyone and everything were all supplied to the press far in advance.

I'm sure no one who counted ever realized I was among the missing.

A small voice inside my head chides me: *Remember, you're not the only one. Theo is among "the missing," too.*

All of the Roosevelts were "missing" for the Ball of the Century. Theo and Alice were too far away and too occupied with legislative matters and Albany society to attend. Hugely pregnant Conie understandably could not be seen in society. Elliott was out of the continent again—Europe, or maybe India—I can't remember which. Bamie and Miss Mittie were both under the weather (a frequent occurrence for them both), "taking the waters" at an out-of-state spa. Aunt Annie Gracie joined their journey to keep them company.

However, the Roosevelts are different. *All* of them. They don't seem to crave—or need—validation from high society. Each Roosevelt seems confident and secure in his or her own worth, just as they stand. They don't need Alva Vanderbilt to validate their existence.

Nor do I. (But still...)

Enough of this.

I will say I'm perversely pleased to see that the *New York Sun* published a *very* stern article, critiquing the Ball's "shocking excesses" when there is still so much "suffering" in this city and outside of the city, too. The Ball of the Century shared the front page of the *New York Times* with the recovery of bodies from the Diamond Coal mine disaster.

Shallow and wasteful or not, this ball is already on its way to becoming a legend of the century. A hundred years (or more) will come and go before anyone fails to remember the Ball of the Century for its over-the-top opulence, extravagance, and style.

Together with the venerable Mrs. Astor, society now has a new co-queen. Miss Alva got what she wanted, and she's already glorying in it—I just know.

No one will ever forget this night. Certainly not me.

THURSDAY

29 MARCH 1883

I hear from Aunt Annie that Henry Abbott, my erstwhile partner for the Star Quadrille, squired another girl around to a different society ball last Friday night.

Now that my father is dead … ever since I "went missing" from the Ball of the Century … I must now dress in full black mourning for at least one year (possibly two).

I can no longer appear at frivolous parties and dances, and as such, Henry no longer has an interest in me.

It's better to learn of his shallowness now than later.

This concludes all I ever wish to say about the Ball of the Century or Henry Abbott … ever again.

Sunday

9 April 1883

Yesterday, Theo made the "principal speech" before the State Legislature on behalf of his pet project, the Civil Service Reform Bill. That's all I have to say about that.

I remain true to my vow: no longer will this journal … or my *life* … be about all things Roosevelt.

But I just *had* to mention it once because it's *such* a noble and worthy cause. I believe in this cause utterly, no matter *who* champions it.

Thursday

April 13, 1883

I see in the *Times* that one Alferd Packer, prospector, is charged and being sent to prison because of cannibalism. No comment.

SATURDAY

28 APRIL 1883

A telegram, first thing this morning, informs us that Corinne Roosevelt Robinson gave birth to an eight pound, two ounce baby boy.

She's named him Theodore Douglas Robinson. (I don't think Doug had very much to say about this matter.) A while back, Conie told me that "all of my children … boys or girls … shall always have Douglas as their middle name, in deference to their father."

That's all I have to say about babies for a while.

FRIDAY

4 MAY 1883

I know I vowed not to mention Theo again, but this is too important not to record in my journal: Theo's Civil Service Reform Bill passed on the very *last day* of the legislative session. I *do*

so admire a man who fights for his principles—
and wins … to the betterment of all concerned!

Thursday morning

24 May 1883

M rs. Emily Roebling, wife of the chief
engineer for design and construction
of the monumental Brooklyn Bridge, carried a
rooster in an open box on her lap (apparently it's
supposed to be a symbol of success) as she was
transported in a carriage across the great bridge
for the very first time. Because her husband
became weakened and ill from working on the
bridge, his highly intelligent wife was his go-
between and acting construction manager for
many years.

Today, after *thirteen years* of seemingly
insurmountable challenges and tragic loss of
human life, the Eighth Wonder of the World is
now complete—New York's Brooklyn Bridge is
finally "open for business!"

The ribbon-cutting to mark the opening of this amazing bridge took place, amid great fanfare and with many dignitaries, at 10 a.m. today.

I plan to walk over the bridge myself very soon … once the initial crowds abate.

How exciting it is to live in these modern times, when most anything can happen and generally does!

MAY 27, 1883

Conie's letter to me arrives this afternoon while I'm out "walking the bridge." Alice Lee Roosevelt *finally* conceived, after two and a half years of marriage. Another Roosevelt grandchild is expected—sometime in February.

February—that horrible month when sad (or even bad) things happen … I feel "stabbed from within," as if Theo were my own husband and he was unfaithful to me.

I must stop this—and stop it now.
I will talk no more of this baby.

TUESDAY

29 MAY 1883

Papa's modest stipend actually loomed larger in our budget than I'd realized. Although we have the modest annuity to sustain us indefinitely, I find that I miss the comforting cushion of Papa's "salary."

Although I don't say anything about it to the others (yet), I'm alarmed at how much prices inch up daily: food of all kinds (no matter how basic), coal for our three fireplaces, natural gas for the Welsbach gas mantles in the ceiling, property taxes rising sharply each quarter (this is *such* an expensive city!), plus the surcharge for trash collection, quarterly water bills from the city, and more.

Two weeks ago, after adding up the bill money due, checking it twice and thrice, it was with real regret and a tingling fear that I had to inform Brooks, the housemaid, that we could no longer afford her. She'd have to go.

Her last day was yesterday. Even Cook's presence in our household hangs on by a thread.

Last night, finally Mamma said it out loud in a bitter voice that cut me deeply: "If only you would acknowledge your *duty* to this family and make a prosperous marriage, be it to Jack Stratton or anyone else, everything would be simply ideal. You're not *that* old, you know. You still can make a good marriage—and you must! But *no*, you persist in remaining selfish to the core. Just because you 'don't want to' … as if *that* were an answer to anything."

I'm ashamed to say we really have it out then, Mamma and I.

We shout, we argue, and both of us cry bitterly. We yell at the top of our lungs. Vitriol flows like acid between us. Em is in the thick of it, an avid bystander and self-appointed referee. But Mamma and I disallow my little sister from getting a word in edgewise.

Finally spent—both of us—I emerge as the unacknowledged winner. I will agree to *no* marriage of convenience and money. I will only marry for love and only when *I* want to—which will probably be never because my chosen partner belongs to another.

I will *not* sell my soul and body just to shore up our family's finances. I'd much rather be poor.

Thursday

31 May 1883

I magine the horror! And the tragedy of such an aftermath...

Yesterday, many people were blithely walking across the new Brooklyn Bridge—not open yet to any vehicles, just walkers at present—when someone started shouting: "It's about to collapse! Run for your lives!"

Others started crying out: "What? It's giving way? Run!"

Suddenly, there was a vast, roaring stampede ... just the same as if it were wild buffalo on the prairies ... only now it was panicked humans. (Later reports said there were no vibrations or movement of the bridge structure whatsoever.)

When the stampeding animals (humans) finally made it to "safety" on either side of the water, it was found that twenty-five helpless human beings were crushed to death. *To death.* What a horrific, wicked, wasteful way to die!

I don't think I'll go walking again on the Brooklyn Bridge just yet ... not until many months pass.

I'll wait long enough to give the human beings of New York City plenty of time to see for themselves that the great bridge is sound.

THURSDAY

7 JUNE 1883

An ancient Asian saying says: The current of life is ever onward. I observe its inexorable flow from my murky backwater.

No more do I rage, cry, and yearn.

I quietly affirm that life is now as it should be: a place and a time where Theo and Alice are *meant* to be together, and so they are.

I, too, am a part of life's current—just *exactly* where I should be. The river flows on. I can honestly reaffirm that my cankerworm of jealousy is dead. Life is the way it is for a *reason*—even if I cannot yet discern it.

Elliott recently returned from India and immediately asked the glamorous, notorious, party girl Anna Rebecca Hall to marry him; she accepted. A December wedding is now slated for the winter high society season.

Rendered nervous by impending fatherhood, Theo—accompanied by his pregnant wife— now spends time at a Catskills health spa, called Richfield Springs. (How he must detest that! He's always abhorred such places.) He writes Conie that the family doctor is making him go "like it or not." Theo says that the place is like a large hotel "for underbred and overdressed girls."

Finally, with great joy and enthusiasm, Theo and Elliott decide they'll head west together to the Dakota Territory Badlands, just east of Montana. "The boys" have big plans for big game hunting. Theo also wants to fully scope out this place where the Old West begins—finally! A dream of his for a very long time.

* * *

Thursday

19 July 1883

Is it my imagination … or are my sketches and paintings (to which I've half-heartedly returned) becoming more skilled and sophisticated? In short, "better?" Is all this "practicing" actually helping? Or am I becoming deluded in my advancing age? Yet to be determined.

Theo is definitely "in the West" right now, and he likes what he sees. Conie writes to tell me of a more alarming situation: Theo has been "bewitched" into putting down a *shocking* sum of money (the sisters hint that it might even be half his entire inheritance) to enter into the red-hot Dakota cattle business with various partners.

Meanwhile, architectural design work begins on the sprawling, spacious new Roosevelt house overlooking Oyster Bay.

As for me? Right now, I'm trying *not* to listen to that wildly popular song in my brain, that mournful ballad by Paolo Tosti, titled "Good-bye:"

What are we waiting for, you and I?

A pleading look, a stifled cry,

Good-bye, forever! Good-bye, forever!

Good-bye, Good-bye, Good-bye!

It kind of makes you think, doesn't it?

JUST BEFORE BEDTIME

THURSDAY

2 AUGUST 1883

I am so lonely.

There. I've said it. It is what it is.

That is, it was what it *was.* More about that in a moment.

Today, I realize that I am tired of relying on myself for, well, everything: comfort, admiration, and affection. I need a warm, loving body lying next to my own—especially in the long, dark nights.

Today, a tiny stray dog with wiry black fur keeps following me, its eyes begging for food as I walk the streets of Little Italy toward my Rudiments of English class, where I assist the regular teacher for an hour, three times a week.

With its pointed ears and small, bat-like face, the dog looked absurdly like a black South American marmoset that I've seen in naturalist sketches.

I can't help it. I decide if this dog is still around waiting by the stoop after class, I will snatch it up and take it home.

And so I do—after first borrowing an old dishtowel from the settlement house in which to wrap and carry the verminous pup. I certainly don't want to find myself later covered in fleas.

The little dog—skin and bones, shivering with nerves yet anxious for food and attention— allows me to pick it up without a whimper. That's when I see she is a girl.

"Schatzi," I announce to no one but myself. The name came out of nowhere, but it suits my little dog. I understand enough German to know the name means something along the lines of "little treasure."

She's treasure indeed. I need her just as much as she needs me.

When I get her home, both Mamma and Em are out at the time, thank goodness, so Mame and I feed the ravenous pup and take her out to do her business. (There isn't much of *that*—not yet, anyway; there will be more, of course, once she starts getting regular feedings.)

Then we take Schatzi to the laundry tubs in the basement scullery. There, Mame and I wash the little dog, first with a light dilution of kerosene in plenty of water to kill the fleas (keeping the solution out of her eyes, of course), then a second bath with mild suds, and finally, a rinse in warm, clear water.

When she and Em return home, Mamma just shakes her head at Schatzi—what *could* I want with such a mongrel creature?!—but once she is assured of the dog's flea-free state, she makes no further protests. Em loves the pup on sight, bless her heart. Now, although I've made up an official bed for the dog—a little nest-bed on the floor beside my own—I can't resist bringing the dog onto the bed beside me.

It's August, and it's plenty warm here on the second floor. The furry pup doesn't need a blanket. I turn onto my right side, wrapping my left arm over her clean, furry, good-smelling little body.

I draw her close to my chest … and then lean over awkwardly to write this journal entry without waking the dog.

My dog.

Finally, I don't feel quite so alone anymore.

THURSDAY

11 OCTOBER 1883

Surprise! Theo's finally back from the Badlands—news to me, but it says so in today's *Times,* so it must be true (ahem).

The paper reports that Theo is already campaigning like a madman for a Republican supremacy in the State Assembly.

Theo must have been home for a while because the article reports that "Mr. Roosevelt is already campaigning by train, by buggy, and also on foot."

How Alice must *hate* that. I can't say as I blame her. *But…*

I'm all too aware that, take it or leave it, love it or hate it, this is just the way Theo *is*. There'll be no changing him at this stage of his life. He must always be going … seeing … doing … striving.

He just can't help himself. Alice will just have to get used to it.

When she married Theo, Alice was most likely unaware of her husband's proclivity for being unable to stay in one place for any length of time.

I know about it—this way that he *is*. I've *always* known about it and learned how to meld myself around it—for all the good it does me now.

MONDAY

15 OCTOBER 1883

I was always taught—by Aunt Annie Gracie herself in her home school, as a matter of fact—that civil rights for all (including former slaves) was both good, noble, and the right thing to do. They even passed national legislation about it in the Civil Rights Bill of 1875.

But now, today, the Supreme Court says that such basic civil rights are wholly unconstitutional. They conclude that individual persons and businesses MAY actually discriminate against other people, just "because."

This can come to no good … I envision storm clouds in the future about this.

SUNDAY

4 NOVEMBER 1883

Earlier this evening, I went to a poetry reading in lower Manhattan to hear the works of one Emma Lazarus, a woman of astonishing intellect with the "courage to act" on behalf of oppressed peoples.

Handsome and wealthy, this single woman of Portuguese-Jewish heritage has an absolutely riveting voice, speaks several languages, and writes prose, poetry, and translations. Plus, she frequently works with Jewish refugees coming to Ward's Island near New York City as they flee Czarist Russia. (Talk about doing good deeds! She puts my paltry offerings to shame…)

When refugees from the Russian pogroms started arriving here, in addition to helping them first hand, Emma was also inspired to write one of the poems she read today: "The New Colossus." She'd just written this poem recently, and tonight, she announced she's donating this poem (a sonnet, actually) to an auction conducted by the "Art Loan Fund Exhibition in

Aid of the Bartholdi Pedestal Fund for the Statue of Liberty" to raise funds to build the pedestal.

It's an inspiring sonnet that talks admiringly about women, but part of the auction money (if enough cash is raised) will go toward having the last couple sentences from the sonnet inscribed on a bronze plaque on the pedestal of the Statue of Liberty, that wonderful gift from the people of France:

Give me your tired, your poor,

Your huddled masses yearning to breathe free,

The wretched refuse of your teeming shore.

Send these, the homeless, tempest-tost to me,

I lift my lamp beside the golden door!

MONDAY

6 NOVEMBER 1883

H oly Hannah, the Democrats won the majority in the State Assembly *yet again.*

It makes me want to stamp my feet and scream. They are such despicable, corrupt, *low lifes!*

But then, I'm well aware that *both* political parties are equally "impure." Bribery is a way of life in the Assembly, so much so that most of the NYC Republican delegation surreptitiously "took the cash" and surrendered their majority for filthy lucre. Aunt Annie Gracie tells me not to worry. Theo refuses to let *anything* get him down. Yesterday, at a new watercolor exhibition at the Met (yes, Aunt Annie still takes pity on me and squires me around town as her companion), she confided to me that "Teedie's position now is stronger than it was last year, enabling him to accomplish *far* more than he ever could have as Speaker of the House. That's because the Democrat who *did* win the majority is surprisingly a gentleman, and he offered our young man whatever he wants in the way of committee appointments. So far, Theo's chosen three: banks, militia, and the powerful cities committee—of which he's already been made chairman ... but of course!"

With verve, skill, and style, Theo is already working up to fourteen hours a day at the Legislature.

Aunt Annie confides that, every morning for a half hour, Theo spars with a young prize fighter in his rooms. "To speed up his metabolism, he says!"

She also confides that, each day, Alice gets larger and larger.

And *larger.*

She's *so* large that she can't receive even female callers anymore.

Aunt Annie divulges that her own sister, Miss Mittie, worries that "something is *really wrong*" with this pregnancy. But she doesn't want to distress the formerly svelte, young wife with her unvoiced concerns, so she says nothing to Alice.

Nothing … yet.

Everyone is just counting the days until that baby can come *out*—the sooner, the better. (*Safely* born, of course, with mother and child both doing well.) Three *months* yet remain before the babe's expected arrival date around

Valentine's Day. From the looks of Alice, that baby could come out right *now*.

There are three more months in which Alice *might* grow to unreal, gargantuan proportions.

Thursday

18 November 1883

Every city in the United States has always used a different time standard, their own "local time"—that is, up until now. There used to be more than three hundred "local sun-times" from which to choose. But this started making the operators of new railroad lines absolutely crazy! They lobbied the government that there *had* to be a "unified time plan" that would offer a "uniform train schedule for departures and arrivals."

So, on this very day, the government is implementing four standard time zones for the continental United States—Eastern, Central, Mountain, and Pacific—at the prodding of the railroads in the United States and Canada. Now the "trains can run on time" because everyone will finally know the locally standard time.

What an eminently sensible idea!

SATURDAY

1 DECEMBER 1883

It's well after midnight. I'm still awake. I can't sleep.

I haven't been able to properly sleep for a long time now, although having dear Schatzi curled under my chin definitely provides some bedtime comfort.

Another society wedding took place this afternoon and well into the night; another glamorous couple united in holy matrimony— this time, it's our own dear boy, Elliott Roosevelt, or "Nell," as Teedie still fondly calls his handsome younger brother.

The ceremony was at the Fifth Avenue Presbyterian Church late this afternoon so Theo could "stand up" for his only brother yet still have time to catch the late train back to Albany.

There were well-dressed *mobs* of people at the wedding. Theo didn't see me, of course, although I definitely saw *him*, the best man, at the altar. That's all right. He wasn't looking for me in any case. Alice, in her engorged state, did not attend.

Miss Mittie was there as mother of the groom, along with her sister, Aunt Annie, daughters Bamie and Conie (I should say Corinne now—she's asked everyone to call her by her proper name, for some unknown reason), along with C's dour husband, Doug Robinson.

And the bride? She's a rich, glamorous society girl and a regular "raving, tearing beauty" named Anna Rebecca Hall.

Both she and Nell are well known among Manhattan's party set.

Everyone hopes that handsome, hard-drinking Nell will now settle down into domesticated matrimony. At the reception, Elliott even said: "You know how a chap like me loves to be ruled over by a beautiful woman!" Anna Rebecca Hall *is* beautiful, incandescently so—as well as being a spoiled brat.

During the reception, the bride said (with a roll of her arresting, hazel eyes), "I hope Nell is not going to form an ideal of me that I shall have to shatter thereafter!" She kept niggling at her groom … saying "I hope you're going to provide me with the excitement I crave—else there'll be hell to pay!"

I've heard around town that Nell's bride is bone lazy and incapable of creating a loving, firm, domestic framework that her new husband desperately needs.

Both of them seldom think of anything beyond parties, bourbon, new clothes, dancing, and dissipation.

After I'd been at the reception awhile, before the dancing even began, I quietly asked a footman to summon me a hansom cab and escaped for home.

Nobody missed my presence—not even me.

WEDNESDAY NIGHT

26 DECEMBER 1883

I t's sunny today, this Boxing Day after Christmas. Brilliant ice crystals cover everything from lampposts to hitching rails.

This afternoon, we four Carows splurge on a hansom cab ride to the after-Christmas reception at the big house (West 57th) presided over (beautifully as always) by the smiling Miss Mittie. The Roosevelt family matriarch always adores a party, especially one of her own.

It was Aunt Annie who invited me, though, together with my reluctant, reclusive family. She did so both as a courtesy and a kindness. If I ever *did* take up swearing (most unlikely), I'd swear that this blessed woman is a sure-enough *angel.* She's always plucking me up from life's backwaters and immersing me, sweetly yet relentlessly, back into the mainstream of life.

Today, I catch a brief glimpse of Alice as Theo (knitted afghan slung over his left shoulder) guides his ponderous wife toward a private back parlor before too many guests make their appearance.

Alice's blue eyes are partially obscured by an ominous, puffy look. He eases her onto a chaise lounge, covers her with the afghan, and tucks it gently around her slippered feet. (I note that her stocking-covered ankles appear gross and swollen.)Theo kisses the top of her head. His look is pitying.

It's cruel of me to even *think* it (let alone say so), but … Alice looks like Humpty Dumpty.

Suddenly, I'm so *ashamed* of myself and my nasty thoughts and overwhelmed by a tidal wave of remorse. For once, I don't envy her the pregnant state she's in—nor the husband who got her that way.

As I move toward Alice, my eyes fix on the weary young woman who undoubtedly just longs for it *all to be over*, Theo exits the room before I can enter. He closes the door behind him, closing me out.

Almost imperceptibly, he shakes his head *no* at me. "She's *so* tired, you see. Poor darling!

Quite understandably so. She'd rather not appear before company while she's still so…"

He doesn't finish his sentence. Anyway, I know what he means.

Leaving Alice alone, I follow Theo back toward the cheerful sound of dishes, goblets, and silverware clinking together, punctuated by plenty of laughter and conversation.

The rest of the reception is both cheerful and instructive; I glean several useful nuggets of knowledge from the party chatter, including the following: Theo and Alice recently sublet their West 45th Street "honeymoon house" to newlyweds Elliott and Anna. They plan to move back to the third floor of Miss Mittie's house so that Alice will have "more companionship" in the last days of her pregnancy. Elliott and Anna already snipe at each other in public. (No surprise there.) Conie is happily enthralled by, and thoroughly engaged with, her firstborn son, the tow-headed Theodore Douglas Robinson the first. She's obviously *less* enthralled by her husband. (No surprise there, either.) Conie plans to stay at Miss Mittie's "for quite a while," without her husband. Mentally and physically, Alice is pretty much at the end of her rope with Theo. Because of his legislative duties, she only sees him on weekends, poor girl. Even an envious old maid like me must feel sorry for her situation. The precious weekends with her husband are now crammed with "unavoidable political entertaining," in which she cannot participate in her present state. I know she *must* long for the lusty, male presence of her husband. I know *I* certainly would. In a corner of the front parlor, Miss Mittie, Aunt Alice, Bamie, and Conie murmur together in low, worried tones— while I listen nearby and make no comment. They talk about Alice.

"Dr. Soames says that she's fine, but Dr. Adler isn't so sure. I'm not sure what to think, something's just *not right*."

I know nothing of pregnancy's vicissitudes, but I can't help but concur. Something's just not right.

FRIDAY NIGHT

11 JANUARY 1884

This morning, Theo introduces three "anti-political-machine" bills in the Assembly. I can't stop smiling, and if Mamma and Em weren't sipping their coffee nearby, I would *shout* with joy!

The *Times* even quotes Theo: "Corrupt machines ultimately govern this city, and I do not consider that to be democratic."

Always, Theo's fearsome goodness propels him forward to do battle with evildoers. My heart can't help repeating the same refrain: *Go, dear heart. Go get 'em.*

WEDNESDAY

16 JANUARY 1884

Yesterday, Theo was named chairman of a special committee to investigate the local government of the city and county of New York. The newspapers even featured a handsome woodcut of him—I see that he's finally cut off those ridiculous side-whiskers! He looks *so* much better now. He's less foppish, more self-assured, and strong.

Newspapermen and Theo's political compatriots *all* respect and admire him. No one condescends anymore. Bamie confides to me that Theo learned to work with all *sorts* of people, "bankers and bricklayers, merchants and mechanics, lawyers and farmers, day laborers, saloonkeepers, clergymen, and prizefighters, and he rejoices in it *all!* You know he can be very funny if he chooses to be, especially in that hilarious, falsetto voice he can do so well!"

Yes, I know his "funny" voice, very well.

"And on a totally different note, I should tell you that your little stray dog … Schatzi, you call her? … isn't a mongrel at *all.*" Bamie nods decidedly. "I recently saw a woodcut of a dog just like her—in *Frank Leslie's Illustrated Newspaper*, it was—and they called it a Belgian Shepherd or Schipperke, bred to go after vermin on Belgian canal barges." Whether Schatzi has a pedigree or not, I couldn't love her better if she was a king's beloved lapdog.

WEDNESDAY

6 FEBRUARY 1884

"Roosevelt on a Rampage!" So reads the headline in today's *New York Times.* These days, Theo pushes hard for investigation of corruption in the New York City government—*all* representatives of the government, Republican or Democrat.

Theo made a major speech yesterday in support of the Mayoralty Bill, which comes up for its second hearing today. "One of his best speeches *ever*," says Bamie, who heard all about it from a political friend and who told me about it at lunch today. How I wish I'd been there to hear Theo's speech!

The press adores him. They love it when Theo whacks the heads off corrupt office-holders in this city.

Monday

11 February 1884

I meet up with Aunt Annie Gracie for lunch at Delmonico's today. She confided to me that Theo told Alice yesterday, "How I hate to leave my bright, sunny, little love, my heart's dearest!" Just before he hops a train—yet again—tomorrow morning, back to Albany.

The Legislature is deep into it now, and Theo can't afford to miss a minute of it.

When a string trio in a sunny corner of the restaurant played a popular new song: "Rock-a-Bye Baby," I can only think: *Indeed!*

Before I can change the subject to one more cheerful for me—i.e., non-Rooseveltian—Aunt Annie prattles on. "Theo hopes the baby will be born on Valentine's Day, the fourth anniversary of the announcement of their engagement. You know how he sometimes gets these 'preternatural' feelings—he just 'knows' Baby will arrive on Valentine's Day, so he trusts there's still time for one more quick trip to Albany to tend to the

Roosevelt Bill. Poor Alice, she doesn't like it one *bit*, and I can't say as I blame her. It *is* awfully close to her due date."

Aunt Annie explains that Alice is especially uneasy because Conie quitted the house for a few days to show off Baby Teddy to Cousin Maud, who now lives in the Bronx. Miss Mittie is also sick abed with a terrible cold—"at least, we *think* it's a cold, and of course, *I* live right close by and stop in most days to see Alice. But at the house, besides the servants, there's only Bamie up and around to check on Alice 'round the clock. Alice's parents moved in yesterday at the Brunswick Hotel, waiting for the baby— naturally, they'll be with Alice a lot of the time. Plus, Elliott and Anna are only a few steps away, so Theo *says* he's not 'overly concerned.' But still, I wonder…"

EARLY ON TUESDAY

12 FEBRUARY 1884

Today, I awake with a feeling of dread—I can't really say why. Maybe it's the unusually oppressive sky.

The entire city is shrouded in a cold, thick, slowly dripping, and oddly brown fog. "Longshoremen are saying it's the thickest fog in twenty years," reports our milkman to Mame when he makes his delivery (late, because of the fog).

Throughout the day, I learn that train service is reduced to an absolute minimum. Even river traffic is cancelled, except for a few ferries venturing out, cautiously in the thickening brown-grayness. All of us Carows stay home today, despite any prior commitments or good deeds that need doing.

The fog makes everything smell execrable— like dung mixed with pungent, sodden ashes. Sticky mud covers the streets. Newspaper boys yell through the fog, "Weathermen predict more foggy, threatening weather."

LATER ON TUESDAY

12 FEBRUARY 1884

G ood thing Theo caught the express train to Albany at dawn today. It must be a relief for the still-asthmatic young man to get out of NYC and back to the bracing cold of a clear blue Albany sky!

When last I heard about Theo from Bamie and Conie, he was a confident, happy man, facing political adversaries with more than three hundred and thirty pages of damning testimony already taken by his Investigative Committee. How he's been looking forward to the prospect of more sensational revelations in the weeks ahead!

He's again making front-page news, and his "Roosevelt Bill" is sure to pass. If only Alice can hold out until Thursday—her due date, Valentine's Day.

If all goes well, Theo plans to personally guide the bill through the House on Wednesday afternoon. To help speed the bill through the Senate, a mass meeting of citizens was called to gather in New York's Cooper Union on Thursday evening.

Things are going *so* well for Theo now that I ... worry.

Divine providence, I urge you ... I *beg* you ... let things go well for dear Theo now. Yes, and for Alice, too.

I pray that destiny arranges itself in the path of the highest and best good for all concerned. Let right prevail ... let right prevail ... let right prevail...

VERY LATE ON TUESDAY

12 FEBRUARY 1884

Someone twirls our doorbell knob at exactly 11:10 p.m. (I checked the clock). I race down the stairs, with my heart beating in my throat.

It's a telegram. *(Oh, dread...)* I search around for (and finally find) a stray coin to give the delivery boy.

The telegram is from Aunt Annie, addressed to me.

I breathe a tiny bit easier, but still ... I open the missive with hands that shake.

Alice. The telegram reads:

AFTER DIFFICULT DELIVERY
MRS ALICE ROOSEVELT
HAS GIVEN BIRTH TO BABY
GIRL (STOP) MOTHER
FEELS APPROPRIATE TO
CIRCUMSTANCES (STOP) BABY IS
HEALTHY (STOP) AUNT ANNIE.

Well!

A daughter ... Theo now has a *daughter.*

I'm awake for hours after this knowledge, my mind racing this way and that. Here I am, writing in my journal at 3:47 a.m.

WEDNESDAY

13 FEBRUARY 1884

I now will recreate on paper the facts of the most awful reality, just as it happened, both for my own sanity and knowledge … and also for that of Theo's daughter when she grows up, if she ever wants to hear a true account of her birth.

And all the rest.

Early Wednesday on 13 February 1884, at the beginning of the morning session of the House of Representatives, assemblymen are seen flocking around Theo and shaking his hand.

In the night, Theo receives a telegram from the doctors, saying Alice gave birth to a baby girl. Theo's telegram is, of course, more detailed than mine from Aunt Annie (who so kindly sent me one, sensing that I'd want to know).

After the initial message, the doctors elaborated in Theo's telegram:

THE MOTHER WAS ONLY FAIRLY
WELL, BUT THAT WAS TO BE

EXPECTED AFTER THE AGONIES
OF A FIRST DELIVERY (STOP).

Theo requests a leave of absence, starting that very afternoon … right after the passage of his second bill.

His compatriots report that he's "full of life and happiness" as he proceeds to "report" fourteen other bills out of his Cities Committee. After all, joy over his new daughter must not be allowed to interfere with his duty to the good people of New York. By late afternoon, a second telegram arrives for Theo. As he reads it, his face suddenly changes. Looking suddenly "worn and frightened," he rushes off to catch the next train south.

At this very moment, Conie (carrying her baby boy) jumps into a hansom cab, which races back to her mother's house after receiving her own second telegram of the day.

Elliott meets his younger sister at the door of West 57th with words of doom: "There is a curse on this house. Mother is dying, and Alice is dying too."

What? Dying? Both of them?

With Grandpa and Grandma Lee staying in the house with Alice long before she took this turn for the worse, Bamie had gone over to Aunt Annie's for a couple of hours. A tragic follow-up telegram catches the women at Aunt Annie's house. Both rush back to Miss Mittie's as fast as they can.

Wednesday by suppertime, it's like a nightmare for Theo to catch a train—*any* train, slow or express—back into the city. The crippling, insidious brown *fog* snarls all traffic into or out of the metropolitan area.

Finally, a train heading south slowly chugs into view. It's one of the slow trains—not an express, but one that makes all of the stops.

With inexorable slowness, the train crawls down the Hudson Valley into the thickening fog that shrouds New York City like a clammy, impenetrable nightmare.

Even in clear weather, the one hundred and forty-five mile journey usually takes five hours. It's anybody's guess how long it will take on this murky evening.

Theo tries not to panic. Only four days and six years ago—also right around the time of Valentine's Day—he jumped on another such slow train into the city in response to another urgent telegram ... arriving hours later to find his father already dead.

It's about 10:30 p.m. when the train finally pulls into Grand Central Depot. Frantically, Theo searches in vain for a hansom cab; none are to be found.

He's going to have to run home on his own.

He barely spots the West 57th Street sign in the denseness of the fog. It looks as if thick brownish-gray curtains are drawn around any ray of light.

He literally feels his way through the fog-shrouded streets to the Roosevelt mansion. When he finally pulls open the front door, the house is dark, except for a glare of gaslight shining down the stairway from an upper floor stairway. Here, finally, he receives the horrific, not-to-be-believed news—from numb, disbelieving Elliott ... sobbing Conie ... horror-struck Bamie ... and grieving Aunt Annie ...

amid the weak wails and die-away moans of Grandma and Grandpa Lee—the news that not only is Alice dying of an ailment called Bright's Disease (kidney dysfunction, who really knows at this point) but that Miss Mittie is *also* dying— dying of typhoid fever, the "dirty water" disease. (This seems unthinkable for Miss Mittie, who always takes two hot baths a day and is ever so spotlessly clean.)

Alice is too far gone to make any gesture of recognition when Theo races up three floors to her side.

At Conie's sobbed request and with her full permission, Aunt Annie directs a stone-faced servant to order another telegram sent. This time, it's a second message—to me.

PLEASE COME NOW (STOP)
HELP US IN OUR TIME OF GRIEF
(STOP) MRS. MITTIE AND ALICE
ARE BOTH DYING.

Shaking all over, I'm out of my nightclothes and into the first dress I come to (black—most of my clothes are mourning garb). Entrusting Schatzi to Emily's willing arms, with a few terse words, I tell my mother and sister what's happening. "I won't be back tonight. Don't worry, I'll be all right with Conie. She—they—need me." Just like that, I'm off and gone … running block after block, by myself in the ominous blackness … feeling my way by instinct in the fog-shrouded night.

At the Roosevelt house, I let myself in without knocking. I'm greeted by Conie's sobs. (Her baby must be up in the nursery in the care of a servant.) I spend much of the first hour just hugging her in futile grief and commiseration.

Finally, I tiptoe down to the kitchen to ask the servants to bring up some coffee and tea—I'll tend to it, once they bring it up.

I don't know what else to do.

Thank goodness, Conie's little son, Teddy, remains asleep; if he were awake, he'd be a handful and a noisy, whining one at that.

But I *do* hear a baby cry, somewhere—high, shrill, and very far away. It's not coming from Alice's room, though.

Abruptly, it stops.

It must be the *new* baby, I'm thinking. A newly hired nursemaid must be sitting in a rocking chair in another darkened room, somewhere in the house, allowing the newborn to suck on one "sugar-tit" after another to quiet its lusty cries.

Silently, I bring cups of tea and coffee around to those who seem physically able to ingest it. (Fortunately, I already know how each individual prefers his or her beverage "fixed.")

Elliott is glad for some coffee, but I see him pour a large dollop of whiskey into his cup with fingers that tremble.

Aunt Annie is glad for her tea, as well; she takes it with her as she goes in to sit beside her older sister's deathbed.

Conie clutches her teacup like a lifeline, still sobbing, as she alternates her time between her mother's bed on the first floor and Alice's room two floors above.

Stone-faced and weary, Bamie sits beside Elliott as they take comfort in each other's presence. Soon, they too will go in to sit beside their dying mother.

I don't know where Grandma and Grandpa Lee might be, and I don't ask.

Theo has not yet left Alice's side.

He doesn't even know I'm here.

Which is just as well.

I sit quietly in a straight chair in a night-black corner of the hallway by the front door.

I just ... wait.

Of the discernible lights on now in the house, a bright gas lamp burns beside Alice's bed on the third floor, even shining a bit down the main stairs. A single candle flickers beside Miss Mittie's deathbed on the first floor. (I learn of this later.) Occasionally, I glimpse a few faint flickers of light from the lower level kitchen—probably when the stairway door is opened or closed.

That is all.

I know that, somewhere in the house, three doctors—all specialists, all who informed the family that the end is imminent for both women—must sit and wait.

There's nothing more they can do.

I'm thinking they're probably in the library, a quiet, first-floor room at the other end of the house, where a single gaslight is probably turned low, yet still burning, as they smoke cigars and quietly drink their brandies.

And give the family privacy.

Waiting to be summoned after the soul departs each body.

I sit in the silent blackness and make not a sound. The family knows I'm here in the hallway if anyone needs me.

Theo keeps holding Alice in his arms (or so I am told—I do not see this). For hours, he sits and holds her. I'm thinking the Lee parents must be with them, too, at least part of the time.

Meanwhile, two floors below, Miss Mittie is dying of typhoid fever.

I hear church bells at Fifth Avenue Presbyterian chime the hours in the darkness.

Elliott himself finally relays a grim message from Miss Mittie's bedside upstairs to Theo, where the latter continues to hold his dying wife in his arms.

I glimpse Elliott's tragic, handsome face as he trudges up the stairs. In the pervasive darkness, he doesn't notice me sitting there. (Which is just as well.)

From two floors up, I hear Elliott's voice, harsh with grief—loud and clear—in the silence of this cursed house: "If you want to say goodbye to Mother, you must do so *now*."

Both brothers descend the stairs with speed, enter Miss Mittie's room—where the rest of the family, except the Lees, keep vigil at her bedside—and the brothers close the door behind them.

I say nothing as I wait in the darkness.

At precisely 3 a.m., in the wee hours of Valentine's Day, 14 February 1884—I hear the church bells, so I know—I also hear a sudden, rising wave of anguish. I know that Miss Mittie must have finally died, with her children and younger sister by her side.

She is … was … only forty-nine years old. Her velvet black hair had not yet a single strand of gray.

(I hear about this a bit later. For now, I don't intrude upon the Roosevelt family's grief. But I tiptoe over to the library—yes, the doctors are still there. I inform them that Miss Mittie has most likely expired. They follow me back to the main hall, quietly tap on Miss Mittie's bedroom door, then enter, and close the door behind them.)

After a long while, I see Elliott open the door of Miss Mittie's room. Both he and Theo step into the dark hallway. Theo puts a hand on Elliott's shoulder—an unusual gesture between these often-at-odds brothers, but these are tragic times. He repeats to Elliott, "There *is* a curse on this house." Elliott nods in undeniable assent and pulls Theo in for a quick hug. Theo hugs him back.

Then Theo heads for the stairway to the third floor where, in bewildered agony, he again takes the unconscious Alice into his arms.

Elliott retreats into Miss Mittie's bedroom. I hear the doctors' baritone voices murmuring indistinctly to the family. (I learn later that one of the doctors inquires of the collective family, "Would anyone like me to give them a strong sleeping draught tonight to help soothe your grief?" Everyone, not surprisingly, assents, replying, "Yes, please do so." I'm sure that Mr. and Mrs. Lee will be similarly medicated— wherever they are.)

I tiptoe to the kitchen stairs and descend to the lower level on noiseless feet. I inform the servants gathered there: Miss Mittie has just passed away, but Miss Alice lingers still.

Several female servants burst into tears. I leave them to their grief, ascend the stairs, and resume my seat in the night-dark hall.

Three hours pass. Whether I doze or remain in a trance, I cannot tell you. Time stands still for me at a time like this.

How odd—the darkness seems to be lifting. I can even see an ormolu clock on a hall table. It's almost 6:30 a.m.

I see gray around the windows. Dawn.

But there's no sun to be seen. I tiptoe to a nearby window just to check. The brownish-gray fog grows thicker than ever.

I think I'm the only one awake in the house—that is, Theo and I. The doctors probably doze in their armchairs, waiting for Alice to pass. Conie, Bamie, Elliott, and Aunt Annie must have sunk into exhausted, medicated sleep, either in their bedrooms or perhaps still in chairs beside their mother's dead body.

I forget where I am and doze, too.

Mid-morning, a sudden rainfall awakens me with a violent start. I run to the nearest window to watch. It's clearing the air! For a full five minutes, the sun shines on the muddy streets and steaming rooftops. The weather seems about to change, but then more clouds and more brown fog cloak the city once more.

People are up and awake now, moving about. I see and hear the doctors.

I answer a rap at the front door. It's the coroner—for Miss Mittie. A doctor must have summoned him while I dozed.

I'm still in my dim, little corner by the front door. Probably (hopefully) folks have even forgotten I'm still there.

What *am* I still doing here, anyway?

I don't really know, except, maybe, I'm waiting for … him.

Just to see him, hear him, or know how he's bearing up. If he can "bear up" at *all,* that is. So, I wait.

Conie finally comes to see me. She is spent, wrung out from crying, but evincing a semblance of peace, at last. "Please *do* keep staying with me, Edie, *do* … at least until Alice … you know…"

I nod and give her an uncharacteristic hug— I'm usually not so demonstrative to girlfriends, but this is a matter of life and death. Seemingly heartened by the embrace, Conie goes to recline on a nearby sofa, while I resume my seat by the front door. I wait.

By noon, the temperature measures fifty-eight degrees Fahrenheit on the kitchen hallway thermometer—and this, in the middle of a February winter!

Suddenly, the humidity becomes intolerable: a muddy, brownish-gray steam bath pervades our being.

It is unbearable.

Still, Theo does not come down from the third floor. Alice must yet live.

Finally, the doctors go up to see Theo—and Alice. They come down, and their exhausted faces tell it all. It can't be long now.

The humidity grows more oppressive by the minute. I want to scream, to cry, but I do not dare. Conie remains prone on the front parlor couch.

I don't know where the others are, and I don't ask.

Then, slowly, but without a doubt, the malevolent fog begins to lift. I watch in wonder out the window as the transformation takes place.

Suddenly, cold, dry air blows in from the northeast. Brown tendrils of fog now dissipate, and the sun shines at last, laughing and clear against a sharp blue sky.

It happens just as church bells strike the 2 p.m. hour at Fifth Avenue Presbyterian.

A guttural cry roars from the third floor. I *know* that Alice died at this very moment of transition.

Conie wakes—*she* heard Theo's cry, too. She comes to stand beside me, where I remain seated, frozen in my straight-backed wooden chair.

I hear the quiet rumble of the doctors' voices from the third floor.

Time passes. How much, I cannot say.

Then, footsteps slowly descend.

It's Theo. Theo, the widower.

He sees me first thing, my chin down as I look up at him … mutely … from the chair. He *yells* at me,

"Get her OUT of here!"

His cry becomes a scream—a bellow of invective, pain, and hatred.

His voice sounds like the savage vengeance of Judgment Day.

He sounds like someone who earnestly wishes that *I* were the dead one—not his beloved Alice.

Conie jumps in surprise.

Bamie, Aunt Annie, and Elliott all hear the screamed bellow, too, and rush to the front hall with haste.

"Get her OUT of here, I tell you—what is she *doing* here, anyway?! I never want to see that woman in this house again. Get her OUT, get her OUT of here, I say. And *never* let her come back here again, *ever!*"

I hear myself whispering between stiff lips, "Oh, I'm so very sorry, I'm so, SO sorry … I'm leaving, I'm going now … So very, VERY sorry."

Conie looks at me with pity and understanding. In a low voice only I can hear, she murmurs, "We'll talk later."

With shocking presence of mind, I manage to snatch my cloak and hood from a coat rack before I fling open the front door and run like a crazy person. I run for home. I run away from that loud—yet still beloved—voice, quivering with hate, pain, grief, and loss, a voice I'll never forget so long as I live.

FRIDAY

15 FEBRUARY 1884

L ast night in the East Village, Cooper Union was thronged with crowds. They're "waiting for young Mr. Roosevelt to rouse the crowd about his latest reform bill," reports the *New York Times* this morning.

It's such a perfect place for Theo's faithful to gather in support of his anti-corruption legislation. A while back, Theo specifically chose Cooper Union, a small, private college of science and art in the heart of the city, as the perfect gathering place for his followers. Cooper Union is probably the only place on *Earth*—and that's no exaggeration—that offers full-tuition science and art scholarships to worthy applicants "independent of race, religion, sex, wealth, or social status, open and free to all."

The *Times* article says the place was "packed with thousands of citizens supporting the final Roosevelt Bill, with a passage through the Legislative Assembly that had been postponed, pending Mr. Roosevelt's return to Albany."

The article went on to relate: "The more-than-usually-intelligent audience included General Grant, ex-Mayor Gracie, Professor Dwight, Elihu Root, Chauncey Depew, and two of young Mr. Roosevelt's uncles, James Roosevelt and Robert Roosevelt."

Although the hero of the New York State Assembly didn't—or couldn't—show up yesterday evening, the hall still resounded with cheers at the very mention of his name. "Whatever Mr. Roosevelt undertakes," asserted Douglass Campbell, the keynote speaker, "he does so earnestly, honestly, and fearlessly."

The resolution in support of the bill was approved by a tremendous, reverberating shout from supporters: "AYE!"

Later today, I learned from Mame (who heard it straight from Miss Mittie's senior housekeeper when she went to pay her respects) that Uncle Jimmy and Uncle Rob already knew about the tragedy but kept silent. The family decided by then not to announce news of the two deaths until Saturday morning, 16 February.

I know they're already planning a double funeral.

Although I must keep to the shadows in the church and not let Theo see me, lest he fly into a rage … I'll still be there.

SATURDAY

16 FEBRUARY 1884

Earlier this morning, I rushed out before breakfast to buy the latest editions of the *Times, World, Herald,* and *Tribune*. Large black headlines in the papers bludgeoned readers with the shocking news: ROOSEVELT SUFFERS DUAL LOSS.

From the *New York World*: "Seldom if ever has New York society received such a shock as yesterday in these sad and sudden deaths. The loss of his wife and mother in a single day is a terrible affliction. It is doubtful whether he will be able to return to his labors."

The *New York Herald* talked more about the two dead women than Theo and his politics.

Miss Mittie was praised for her "brilliant powers as a leader of a salon, high breeding, and elegant conversation." Alice was praised for "her beauty, as well as the many graces of her heart and head."

On Friday, in Albany, the Legislative Assembly paid an unprecedented tribute to its stricken member by unanimously declaring an "adjournment of work" in sympathy for Theo's tragedy.

The funeral is slated for tomorrow, Sunday, 17 February ... at the very same church with bells that tolled the hours on Wednesday night in the darkness, tolling (in my mind) for Miss Alice and Miss Mittie.

Dare I attend the dual funeral—after being savagely screamed at to "Go AWAY!" by Theo?

How could I not attend?

LATER ON SATURDAY

16 FEBRUARY 1884

I 've never seen anything like it.

Today, Fifth Avenue Presbyterian Church is packed with more than two thousand people. For some, it is standing room only.

Thankfully, I arrive three hours early—alone. Even so, I am lucky to snag a tiny portion of a pew on the mid-left side of the church. (I dare not move my arms for fear of elbowing people on either side of me.)

Uniformed policemen maintain order and decorum as hundreds *more* attempted to enter the church. Many—*far* too many—stand in the side aisles. Finally, the police effectively close the building to additional mourners.

Amid the throngs, I can barely see the pinpoint heads of the Roosevelt and Lee families in the two front rows.

There's Elliott and his bride, Anna (who was *not,* I noticed early on, among the mourners at the Roosevelt home Wednesday night). Anna

Hall Roosevelt looks stunning in black gabardine with glossy, black fur trim.

There's Conie and, oh yes, Doug Robinson, right next to her; he must have come up on the train as soon as he heard.

Beside them, Bamie is dressed in a deep olive drab—strange color choice—but the upper part of her left arm is covered by a black band of mourning; her black hat is fitted with a long, crepe veil.

Aunt Annie Gracie and her husband, Jim Gracie, sit beside her. Aunt Annie also wears a black, crepe veil.

In the right-hand front pew, I glimpse Mr. and Mrs. Lee—"Grandpa and Grandma" Lee since Alice gave them their first grandchild—surrounded by Alice's many siblings, aunts, uncles, and cousins. Then, I finally glimpse Theo in the midst of the Roosevelt clan.

It has to be Theo's bowed head, with the reddish-brown, slightly wavy hair, small ears, fitted so closely against his skull; it just *has* to be him. It is.

Though all around him continue to weep (for the most part) silently, I can make out that Theo sits, white-faced and expressionless, like an automaton. He seems not to know who or where he is or what's even happening in his life. It's a merciful blankness, perhaps.

Suddenly, a loud swell of the organ commences with the popular new hymn "My Faith Looks Up to Thee," and the famous, kindly, and popular preacher Dr. Hall begins the funeral service.

At the altar, two rosewood coffins are positioned side by side, each covered with sprays of white roses. Silently, I bid goodbye to Alice Lee Roosevelt and Martha Bulloch Roosevelt.

I can scarcely hear Dr. Hall, so many people are sobbing during the simple, dignified service. He can hardly control his *own* voice as he compares the "sad but unsurprising death of a forty-nine-year-old widow" with the "strange and terrible" fate that snatched away a twenty-two-year-old young wife and mother.

Openly and audibly, Dr. Hall weeps now, especially when he concludes the service with,

"Most of all, I pray for *him* … of whose life Alice has been so great a part. May he address himself afresh to the duties that God hath ordained for him."

The funeral concludes with the hymn "Sunshine in My Soul"—most likely at the request of Alice's parents, who always called their eldest daughter Sunshine.

The brief burial ceremony is by invitation only—just for family members and a very few close friends. (Not me.)

Mittie and Alice will be buried in adjacent graves at Greenwood Cemetery in Brooklyn.

I step back into a small alcove, allowing the exiting throngs to pass around me. I want … I need … to see Theo just one more time. (Without him seeing me.)

My dearest one seems so stunned and dazed. He knows not what he says or does. I'm glad to see his sisters guiding him gently about, in love and grief, taking care of him like a child.

TUESDAY

19 FEBRUARY 1884

Early this morning, Conie sends one of her "hall boys" to my house with a note, telling me "the coast is clear" and to please come over to see her today.

The note also says Theo took the first train back to Albany this morning.

He's back to *work*.

I walk at a speedy clip to the Roosevelt house. As I walk, I wonder: is he still mad at me? Did he really mean all of that venomous vitriol?

Will he hate me forever?

When I finally reach West 57th, Conie looks beyond exhausted and deprived of sleep.

Her words come out softly and slow.

"Can you imagine … before he left for the train, Teedie told me he was going to … going to … literally work himself to *death*. If he can. And if he keeps on living—despite his best efforts to obliterate himself—he plans to work *so hard* that it will 'mercifully blur' his pain. If it were only that easy…"

We're both quiet together for a while before Conie speaks again. "I still can't believe it all really *happened*. It still seems a ghastly fever dream ... and if it's ghastly to me, just *think* what it must be like for Theo."

That does not bear thinking about.

After this somber exchange, Conie appears to rouse herself into a greater semblance of normality. Bamie (no doubt hearing our voices) comes downstairs to join us. I don't know where any of the others are, and right now, I don't care.

Thank goodness for the servants—especially at times like this. I think of Baby Lee's nursemaid, augmented by the new (and highly essential) wet nurse, plus little Teddy Robinson's nursemaid—all are literal godsends for the rest of us. Little Ted is a demanding toddler, and newborn Baby Lee seems to cry incessantly. (No one dared call the new baby Alice while Theo was in the house; he couldn't bear hearing the name Alice spoken, although it is the baby's true name.)

Conie and Bamie relate to me the chronology of events after the graveside service, and I'll relate them now to *you*, dear Woman's Journal:

Sunday 17 February — Baby Lee is christened this afternoon, the day after the funeral. The newborn is officially placed in the care of her Auntie Bamie. Now aged thirty and an inveterate spinster (even more so than I am), Bamie experienced the *only* happy event of the entire nightmare scenario—she now has a beautiful new baby to care for and love.

Baby Lee is baptized by the same Dr. Hall who conducted yesterday's funeral. At the christening, Theo remains stunned, dazed, and unable to understand anyone's condolences. He shows no interest in the baby whatsoever. He tells Bamie the baby is hers to bring up now, "better than I could ever do." Theo calls the infant Baby Lee because he can't bring himself to speak her true name, Alice.

Monday 18 February — Theo's grief seems even keener today than yesterday. Bamie, Conie, and Elliott are frightened to death on his behalf. Endlessly, Theo paces his bedroom—the one he shared with Alice—where he continues to emit periodic exclamations of pain. The family is afraid he's losing his mind.

Bamie explains to me, with a quaver in her voice, "What he was *really* doing, *I* think, was trying to dislodge Alice Lee from his soul, like a lion tries to drag a spear from its flank. He tells us that he *must* suppress her memory until … and I quote him … 'the memory is too dead to throb.'"

Though Theo is stunned by grief, he's still strong enough to make a firm decision about the Roosevelt houses: "Sell them both. *Now.*"

A real estate agency is immediately contacted—Uncle Jimmy Roosevelt knows a reputable man. All initial paperwork is signed that afternoon to list both houses for sale. Goodbye, West 57th … goodbye to the newlywed house, too.

Although I shouldn't, I can't help but ask the girls: "But your house … *this* house … won't you miss all of the good memories you made here?"

Bamie's reply is surprisingly brusque. "They weren't *all* good memories, you know. Ever since Father died, Mother has been running through his money like a spoiled child—so heedless and reckless. All those lavish soirees and receptions, banquets and balls, the live orchestras that came to play for guests, even the new livery for the footmen were fancier than for any English royalty, I swear! Truth be told, Father's bank account has been looted by his own widow, and that's a fact. It's time we put a stop to it—especially now, when the estate will soon be divided up four ways. As for me, *I* have neither the time nor inclination to keep up with the Astors, Vanderbilts, and their ilk. With my money portion, I'm going to look for a fashionable but much *smaller* house, perhaps something on Madison Avenue and hopefully near a park, where I can wheel Baby Lee in a perambulator."

I shoot a look at Conie. Her guilty countenance and silence seem to add her own assent.

Apparently, life at West 57th has not always been so safe, omnipresent, and rosy with the Roosevelt fortune as I'd blithely assumed.

And now, today…

Tuesday 19 February — In the dark before dawn, Bamie helps Theo pack a valise with clothes for his return to Albany. Theo tells his family before he boards the train, "There is nothing left for me in this life, except to try to live so as not to dishonor the memory of those I loved who have gone before me."

FRIDAY

22 FEBRUARY 1884

Another thing Theo said to Conie before leaving for the train—I forgot to write it yesterday: "The keenness of joy and the bitterness of sorrow are behind me now since the light has gone out of my life."

Before he left for Albany, Theo wrote two brief valedictories about Alice: one for the family only and one for limited circulation among friends.

Now that he is back in Albany, Conie allowed me to read them both. I copied them out, there at their house, and I include them here.

Both sisters doubt that their brother will ever mention Alice's name aloud again. *I* very much doubt that Theo will ever forgive me … never, ever, ever … just for being alive, while Alice is not.

"She was beautiful in face and form, and lovelier still in spirit. As a flower she grew, and as a fair beautiful young flower she died. Her life had been always in the sunshine; there had never come to her a single sorrow and none ever knew her who did not love and revere her for the bright, sunny temper and her saintly unselfishness. Fair, pure, and joyous as a maiden; loving, tender, and happy as a young wife; when she had just become a mother, when her life seemed to be just begun, and when the years seemed so bright before her—then, by a strange and terrible fate, death came to her. And when my heart's dearest died, the light went from my life forever."

"Alice Hathaway Lee. Born at Chestnut Hill, July 29, 1861. I saw her first on October 18, 1878. I wooed her for over a year before I won her. We were betrothed on January 25, 1880, and it was announced on February 16. On October 27 of the same year, we were married. We spent three years of happiness greater and more unalloyed than I have ever known fall to the lot of others. On February 12, 1884, her baby was born, and on February 14, she died in my arms. My mother died in the same house, on the same day, but a few hours previously. On February 16, they were buried together in Greenwood Cemetery. For joy or sorrow, my life has now been lived out."

TUESDAY

26 FEBRUARY 1884

J ust twelve days after losing his wife and mother, Theo is now also bereft of his homes. The West 57th house was sold early today. A surprisingly good offer for his "cozy little house" on West 45th Street came in early this afternoon. (I dropped off jars of Mame's homemade marmalade for Conie, Bamie, and Aunt Annie, so I learned the news first hand.)

The family accepted both offers. Now, they have until 30 April to vacate both houses. Straightaway, Bamie sent a telegram about it to Theo at the Legislature in Albany.

Theo quickly telegraphed back, asking Bamie to "please divide everything up and clear it out as you see fit. Although I'll return to West 57th to see to my things, I do not wish to return to the house I shared with my bride."

It's good Bamie is so efficient in the midst of pervasive sorrow ... so wise and tender, yet ruthlessly efficient.

LATER ON TUESDAY

26 FEBRUARY 1884

I t finally came! A *telephone* of our very own—I had it on prepaid back-order for ages, but now it's *here*, installed by two workmen late this afternoon.

The intimidating yet exciting device hangs in our back hallway. It looks oddly like a shrine—a large, oaken, rectangular shrine. A black ear-piece for "listening" hangs from a cord on the device's left side. Atop the wooden box, two brass circles clatter and ring like a tiny fire alarm when someone calls. The speaking tube protrudes from the device's middle, much like a goose sticking his neck out of a box. On the right side, a magneto generator, hidden inside, is briskly cranked by hand so it can finally "connect." There's even a rotating "number dial" below the speaking tube—yes, I splurged on a fancy model with this extra adaptation. (I figure we can always skimp on eggs and bread for a while.) The number dial allows me to "dial direct" all on my own, without first talking to "Central."

No longer must I rely on human messengers running back and forth. Nor do I have to resort to telegrams … odious, ominous notes that they are! I can just call anyone I want, whenever I want—providing they have a telephone, too. In midtown Manhattan now, most of our friends have one. It's such a relief for the Carow family to finally catch up with everybody else. Yet ... these marvelous telephones, alas, come with such *ugliness*. The hideous rat's nest of *hundreds* of overhead telephone wires, obscuring and even obstructing so many New York streets, is such a blight on the neighborhoods now ... so much so that city officials are now under constant pressure to "bury the lines!" The officials harrumph and continue to refuse, of course, saying it's "far too expensive." Eventually, they'll have to bow to public pressure; it's getting ridiculous. In the meantime, I revel in the ease and convenience of this technological wonder of the 1880s. What fast times we live in ... and how I *do* enjoy it!

WEDNESDAY

27 FEBRUARY 1884

I called Conie this morning—yes, I actually got the intimidating device to *work* for me, despite the many steps one must remember in proper order!—just to tell her and Bamie that we finally have a telephone in the house.

Conie's reply supplied me with an earful:

"Theo is working *so* punishingly hard—I'm afraid it's going to kill him! He commutes constantly because he has two jobs now—State Assemblyman in Albany on Tuesday, Wednesday, and Thursday—and *then* he comes into the city to be the Chairman of the Corruption Investigation Committee on Friday, Saturday, and Monday. He stays at a hotel—it would be too hard on him to ever sleep in this house again. Speaking of sleep, he pretty much only has Sundays to rest his brain, but he seldom even does *that* because he confided that he 'mostly just sleeps on the trains.' At night, though, whether he's in a hotel or his flat in Albany, he mostly just paces the floor all night long."

Ah, my poor darling! What can I say to this?

"But he *can't* go on like this…" Feebly, I state the obvious. "It's going to kill him."

Conie readily assents: "Yes, it *will*, but he refuses to speak of his grief to the family. He *must* work himself to exhaustion—or go mad."

With empathy and my own discomfort, I rapidly conclude this conversation. It's true—all of it. What more is there to say?

THURSDAY

28 FEBRUARY 1884

Conie received a letter from Theo this morning with news she *knows* I'd want to hear. Thank the blessed telephone for making it possible!

"Theo says he read this front-page article in the *Times* about 'Dressed Beef in the West.' It's some newfangled business angle about new methods of raising cattle in the West—he enclosed the article with the letter. The man behind it all is a French marquis—yes, here it is, the Marquis de Mores. There's a woodcut portrait of him with the article. Only twenty-six years old himself, he's wealthy and handsome as a Greek god. Just right for *you*, Edie! Only, I'm sad to say, he already has a wife, Medora. Theo seems intrigued by this cattle business angle … says he's going to check into it … and *I* say, thank *Heaven*—it's his first sign of interest in *anything* since … you know."

An interest other than sickness, loss, and death has to be a positive sign. Right?

S<small>ATURDAY</small>

1 M<small>ARCH</small> 1884

For some reason—known only to God and Theodore Roosevelt II—Theo just signed the go-ahead papers to start construction of a country house on his property overlooking Oyster Bay.

Bamie says it's going to cost $22,135, for starters—a staggering amount. I hope he'll have something left of his inheritance once he pays this off. It makes my head hurt just to think about it. Usually I'm such a tight-fisted bookkeeper, and dear Theo has never had much thought in his head about money—any money at *all*: the making of it, spending it, keeping it, or saving it. It just never occurs to him to think about money.

He's always had so much ready money, close at hand, that he's never *had* to think about money. It was just always there.

And now…?

FRIDAY

APRIL 18, 1884

I see myself in the entryway mirror: a plain, pale-faced woman all in black. Suddenly, I feel so *very* weary. 1884 brought *so* much death, sorrow, weariness … so many who have "gone on ahead of us"—dear Papa, Miss Mittie, Alice, and even Jack is gone from my life (by distance, if not by death).

I can't help thinking this *very* selfish thought: *How I miss Papa, colorful dresses, activity, and action—and how dearly I miss a good Broadway show!*

Mourning or not, I can't help myself. I telephone Aunt Annie Gracie and ask: "Might you be up for a Broadway show this evening?"

"Indeed I am!" she assured me. (If she were a *Ragged Dick* newsboy, she might reply: "You betcha I am!")

We decided on a new David Belasco play at Madison Square Theater entitled *May Blossom*, a drama of romance and betrayal set before and during the American Civil War.

As we watched the drama unfold before us, I felt a soothing sense of life returning stir within me. Life indeed is *not* over yet—not for any of us, especially me.

SATURDAY

19 APRIL 1884

Great Scott (whoever *he* might be) and Holy Hannah! Why has no one told me about this before? The lead story in the 19 April issue of *Harper's Weekly* features the bipartisan reform team of Theodore Roosevelt and New York Governor Grover Cleveland.

I start to read the article before I even pay for it at the news agent's shop.

A very noble pen-and-ink drawing by artist Thomas Nast shows the two men working side by side. A young Theo stands beside Cleveland's desk, where he steadies a huge, bound packet of legislative bills with his right hand, while the older man, Governor Cleveland, signs them, seated, at the other end of the desk.

The headline reads "Reform Without Bloodshed." A subhead adds: "Governor Grover Cleveland and Theodore Roosevelt Go about Their Good Work."

Theo looks somber as he gazes toward the governor, while Grover Cleveland's gaze is pinned on the far distance.

SUNDAY

27 APRIL 1884

- *NEW YORK WORLD:* "ROOSEVELT ON A RAMPAGE: WHACKING THE HEADS OFF OFFICE-HOLDERS IN THIS CITY"

NEW YORK SUN: "MR. ROOSEVELT'S HARD HITS: MAKING A LIVELY ONSLAUGHT ON NEW YORK'S ALDERMEN"

NEW YORK HERALD: "TAMMANY DEFEATED: MR. ROOSEVELT'S BRILLIANT ASSAULT ON CORRUPTION."

On the telephone, in a voice that betrays her worry and empathy, Conie tells me her brother is running on "nervous energy alone," with very little sleep or food.

He's trying to outrun his grief as far and fast as he can.

WEDNESDAY

30 APRIL 1884

Hardworking Theo enjoys nationwide adulation right now. Yes, I'm pasting a mountain of articles and clippings about him into my (very private) scrapbook.

He's the man of the hour now, and so much more. The *New York Times* calls him "the victor, the wearer of all the laurels." The *Evening Post* calls him "the most successful young politician of our day."

Even Theo's former tutor, Arthur Cutler, tells Bamie (who, of course, later tells me), "TR's reputation is national now, and even to those of us who know him, it is phenomenal! Whatever the future may have in store for him, no man in the country has begun his public career more brilliantly." Young Mr. Roosevelt's life is so full and vital—even if his heart is breaking—and nothing can stop him now.

I can't help comparing his life to *my* life— my endless series of teaching small classes (at no pay) at a settlement house, usually Commercial

English to young women from Hungary and Poland; making more sketches and paintings, each one growing more sure and confident in skill and execution; long daily walks with Schatzi; helping to cook Sunday nights at the Newsboys' Lodging House; going to the theater with Fanny Smith Dana, Aunt Annie Gracie, and sometimes the Roosevelt sisters and even my own sister Em; and knitting on rainy afternoons with Mamma and Em in the back parlor.

It's a respectable life, yes … but still, it's a strange sort of half-life, like that experienced by a shade, a shadow, or a spirit … or, more likely, that of an automaton—proper and worthy but still not fully alive.

Theo's still in pain, but at least *he* knows he's *living*.

What in God's name am *I* doing?

There's a life for me out there somewhere, I just *know* it.

But how do I ever find it? And where?

THURSDAY

1 MAY 1884

At last! All those stalwart workers—the 10,000 who marched in the first Labor Day parade last September and many more who supported them from the sidelines—finally received their first big break: the Federation of Organized Trades and Labor Unions in the United States now proclaims the "8-hour workday." No more compulsory 12-hour days with nose to the grindstone!

May the 8-hour workday soon sweep the country and become the norm! I remember one of Papa's brothers telling us about how (in his own youth) it was commonplace for all men to work a full day every Saturday, too (in addition to Monday through Friday), starting at 6 a.m. and ending at 6 p.m.. With only Sunday left, during which to "pray and rest"—there was little to *no* time left in the week for play. I don't think this is what God had in mind myself...

TUESDAY

30 MAY 1884

N*othing* can stop Theo now, except himself…

Today, he made a statement to both the Assembly and the newspapers: "As of the conclusion of this session of the Legislature, I'm resigning my seat as a New York State Assemblyman and will not seek a fourth term. My troubles over the past year require that I make a clean break in my life. I purchased a ranch near the town of Medora in the Badlands country of Dakota Territory, and, at this time, I shall secure the change I need by going into the cattle ranching business." He's going away, perhaps forever.

He's making a new life. So must *I*. But with *what?* Believe me, I'm looking, truly looking. *There has to be a way*. There has to be something new and different…

WEDNESDAY

31 MAY 1884

Over the telephone, Bamie reads me a letter Theo wrote to the editor of the *Utica Morning Herald*. (He sent his sisters a copy of the printed letter in the paper.)

I wish to write you a few words just to thank you for your kindness toward me, and to assure you that my head will not be turned by what I well know was mainly "accidental" success. Although not a very old man, I have yet lived a great deal in my life, and I have known sorrow too bitter and joy too keen to allow me to become either cast down or elated for more than a very brief period over any success or defeat. I will not stay in public life unless I can do so on my own terms ... and my ideal, whether lived up to or not, is rather a high one. For very many reasons, I will not mind going back into private life for a few years. I feel tired and restless. For the next few months, I shall be in Dakota Territory, and I think I shall spend the next two to three years in the Far West—and there will be plenty of work to do writing.

Sincerely yours,
Theodore Roosevelt II.

I am restless *too*, Theo. I still carry my love for you, always, within my heart. My secret that everyone else has no doubt forgotten.

I doubt you'll ever come back from your new cowboy life.

I don't want to run away. I want to run *toward* something for a change—something new for my family and me … somewhere warm and welcoming … some place where we all can be happy and, yes, useful … yet someplace we can afford.

Is that asking too much?

Thursday

1 June 1884

Bamie bought herself a house! It's a not-very-large but still elegant, three-story brownstone at 422 Madison Avenue. When (and if) Theo ever comes back to New York to visit family, this is where he will stay as his "base of operations" for what remains of his east coast life.

Conie and Doug Robinson also own a townhouse nearby. Even Elliott and Anna, still tumultuous in their relationship, live just a few short blocks away.

Early on this gorgeous June evening, Bamie's "open house" party surges and swirls in boisterous conversation. Laughter, food, and flowers are everywhere throughout the house—each conversation seems louder than the one before. Shrill laughter flows easily from room to room.

After standing, chatting, and *smiling* for so long, my face hurts. My head aches. Shooting pains stab at my insteps. *Enough* of this … I move toward one of Bamie's private back parlors. There, I slip behind a fortuitously situated Chinese screen, where I sink into a lime-green velvet chaise secluded behind it. Even here, I can't get away from the noise. More footsteps and chatter precede the approach of more people, closer to my secret hideaway.

"Oh, but it's absolute heaven!" a middle-aged matron gushes to her friend. (At least, she sounds like a middle-aged matron; I can't see her, so I don't know for sure.) Thank goodness they can't see me behind the screen, or I'd have to be polite and talk with them. I remain in seclusion and scarcely breathe so as not to give my presence away.

"And it's *ever* so much more affordable than anything north of 35th Street," the matron adds.

Another lady sounds incredulous. "You say this pensione actually has four bedrooms? For under forty-two American dollars per month?"

"Yes, and the weather is *delicious* nearly all of the time. It's the seaside influence, you know. There is scarcely any need to buy coal.

Fruit, vegetables, beef, and most *everything* can be bought there for pennies on the dollar. There are cheap wages for servants, too, but still considered very respectable by local standards. By *Manhattan* standards, though, you can live so *well* there for a mere pittance."

Her companion still has a few doubts about this Garden of Eden—wherever it is.

"But all of those foreigners … wouldn't you miss your own kind after a while?"

The middle-aged matron laughs, peal upon peal of delighted retort. "But our own kind are already *there!* Hundreds of them, perhaps thousands, already living there and loving it, all up and down the coast. I tell you, Ardelle, on even a very small annuity each month, you could live there like a *queen!*"

Behind the Chinese screen, I am rigid with attention.

This is what the four forlorn females in our little family need. This is what I *want* for us; this is what we must *have.*

But where is it? I pray that one of the women will utter the name of this fabulous place, specifically. She does—kind of. Well, close enough. I can do the rest of the research on my own.

"You just can't beat the Italian Riviera, especially around La Spezia. Costs are still very reasonable there, much more so than Positano."

Italy. Of course.

By this time next year, we could be smelling orange blossom–scented air.

Italy! Mamma, Em, Mame, and me—what on earth would *they* think?

Will they fight me on this? Think I'm crazy?

I think of my favorite poet, Elizabeth Barrett Browning, and how moving to Italy—and finding love—changed her entire life.

I'm going to spring it on them early tomorrow morning, after I sleep on it first, just to be sure.

I'll brook no arguments. I'm selling our house and moving to Italy, come hell or high water.

And *they* are coming to Italy *with* me.

MONDAY

2 JUNE 1884

"Mame, pour yourself a coffee and sit down with us, please—and have some toast. I've a serious topic to discuss. One that cannot wait."

Seated for breakfast at the dining room table, Mamma and Em look warily at me while Mame takes a seat.

Trepidation is evident in their eyes. They sit and wait like obedient pupils as I begin my campaign.

"We all know Manhattan living grows more expensive every day. As they say, it's the *inflation.*"

(*No* one can argue with *that*, least of all we Carows, who always lived "on the edge.")

"Even with the inheritance annuity from Grandfather Tyler, it's still tough—and getting tougher all the time—for us to meet all of our financial obligations."

Seeing Em's glazed look, I clarify: "The butcher, the Chinese laundry, gas bill for the lights, the telephone bill, the grocers, and paying for deliveries of hard coal for the heaters and soft coal for the fireplaces. But mostly, it's the New York City property taxes we owe. They're climbing *so* steeply now, ever since the city agreed to bury the telephone lines. One of these days, not long from now, our modest annuity of five thousand a year won't be enough. *Plus,* there's still a good-sized *mortgage* on this place, as you well know."

I remind everyone of this shameful fact by giving them all an arch look—not quite an eyeroll, but something very much like it.

"Try as we might, we're no closer to paying it off than we were last year. Truth be told, we haven't been trying very hard either because it takes every bit we can scrape together just to keep on as we are, let alone get ahead in any way and pay off that blasted mortgage."

Mamma's careworn face crumples, suddenly, into a choking sob. Then another, and another.

I should never have said the shocking word "blasted"…

Mamma takes in a deep, shuddering sigh: "But what are we supposed to *do* about all this, Edie? Get a *job*?" (She speaks the word as if it implies entering into prostitution.) Even working at a so-called respectable job—such as a lady's paid companion, salaried school teacher, or starting up a boarding house—would instantly cast us into outer darkness socially. There'd be no coming back from *that*.

Em pipes up, "I suppose we could always move to the country, a farm maybe, where things cost less, and we could grow our own food." She makes surprising sense for my sister.

I seize the moment.

"You're right, we *must* move on—and soon—but *not* to a farm."

My three forlorn females look from one to another. "Then where, exactly?"

My answer leaves them speechless: "*Italy.*"

In various tones and pitches, the three women screech back to me: "*Italy?!* What in the *world*—"

You'd think I'd said Egypt or Estonia, Mauritius or … Mars.

I plunge into my sales pitch—loud, fast, and firm.

I suffer no nonsense today. I suffer no fools gladly, either.

I make it clear that *all* of us could do with a change, a new horizon, a fresh start in a new world—that is, a world that's new to *us*, even if its civilizations are thousands of years old.

Suddenly, their eyes are wide and bright, sparkling in anticipation of pleasure and possibility.

No one gets a word in edgewise as I enumerate the advantages of moving to Italy— which are many—and the disadvantages— which, from what I can see, are *none* (except for the fact of probably never seeing Theo again, but I don't bring up this painful subject).

When I finish pontificating, we all start chattering at once—noisy, happy magpies with a new lease on life.

"Remember," I remind my family, "nothing is really holding us to this house—except for the mortgage. This house has no family history for us, nothing like that. If we sold it for good money and paid off the mortgage, we would *still* make a handsome profit that would easily pay our passage to Italy—second class, but still very nice—on an ocean liner. Plus, we'd still have money enough to ship over all our favorite pieces of furniture, and—"

Mamma speaks up in a quavery, old-lady voice.

(With a pang, I realize how *old* she's getting … and so quickly, too, what with boredom, penury, and hopelessness pressing in against the Carows on all sides.)

"I'll move to Italy under *one condition.*" Mamma's demand hangs in the air—quiet but implacable.

We all look at her soberly.

"And that condition *is* … we spend some of that house money to visit London first, *before* going on to Italy. I want to spend all summer and all of the fall months in a respectable lodging house in London, so I can visit with my extended family there."

Sure! Why ever not? Anything to make the forlorn females come around to my way of thinking.

I'm twenty-three, going on twenty-four now … well past my "first youth," as the old saying goes. By virtue of my knowledge, courage, and determination, I silently appoint myself official head of the Carow household, not just in drudgery and duties but in all aspects from this day forward.

I stand and pound my small fist on the dining table like a man. "Dealt with and *done!* Mamma, Em, Mame … it's agreed then, and it's official. We're moving to Italy, with a detour to London first, just as soon as we can sell this house." Just like that, I changed the vibration pattern of our polite, fusty, and lonely days forever. Not a moment too soon.

FRIDAY

6 JUNE 1884

In the days that follow, I'm careful to caution my family, "We're *not* putting up a For Sale sign for all the world to see and comment on. Instead, we'll just list it with a reliable, discreet sales agent. We don't need all the world knowing and commenting about our private business." (Certainly *not* the agent that Theo and family used to sell the Roosevelt homes.) "I'll ask Mr. Cruikshank for the name of a reputable agent," I tell the forlorn females. (Mr. Cruikshank is the highly respected money manager of Mamma's annuity from Grandfather Tyler.)

I'm careful to caution Mamma, Em, and Mame: "Remember, should our Italy plan start becoming ... difficult ... I don't want our plans known to *anyone* yet—even to the Roosevelt sisters. Everyone gossips *so* horribly these days, and usually, nine-tenths of what is put forth as the gospel doesn't prove to be true. Let's let everyone think we're just planning a long, leisurely trip to Europe and leave it at that."

(How we would *pay* for such a trip is another matter—one that is none of their business.)

I know I'll scarcely sleep tonight, bubbling over as I am with the happiness of new possibilities. Not about a new man—no. I don't want *that*. I don't even think about it.

I just want a whole new life—and I aim to get it.

TUESDAY

10 JUNE 1884

I don't tell my forlorn females this, but I suspect it's going to be devilishly *difficult* to sell this house. It may take months, possibly even *years*. (Oh Lord, anything but that!)

The house itself? It's fine, for the most part, and it makes a *grand* first impression on guests, with our high-ceilinged front parlor decked out with Mamma's elegant furnishings, part of the wedding trousseau from her father nearly a quarter-century ago. The rest of the house is far more modest and plain, though—almost ridiculously so. The main detriment to the sale of our house for good money is its *location*.

We're located perfectly equidistant between respectable neighborhoods to the west and a depressing welter of "dodgy bits" and outright slums to the east. We live uncomfortably close to saloons, gambling parlors, opium dens, and several houses of soiled doves on the east side.

Our neighborhood is, how shall I say it, "in transition." Who will pay top dollar for a house in a neighborhood location that is dubious (at best) and possibly degenerating (much worse)?

I refuse to think about this just now. It will sell. It *must* sell—to somebody, somewhere.

I'm talking some brave, bold talk these days, but inside, I'm desperately afraid of making a fool of myself. Maybe this is all a crazy idea, foolish and ill-advised.

That's why I don't want to tell the neighbors (not yet) nor inform our Tyler relatives, and I *especially* don't want to tell Conie and Bamie— they're my friends but too shrewd by half.

Hardly anything gets past them in the gossip department.

Tomorrow, I'll go to the Office of the Italian Consulate to track down names and mailing addresses of Italian Riviera "pensiones"— especially those favored by American expats—for possible long-term vacancies, starting the spring of 1885. It's almost overwhelming, the amount of research and downright elbow grease it's going to take to get the four of us, and much of our furniture, shipped safely over to Italy. Assuming, of course, that we can sell the house…

Even if our house sells quickly (a dream!), I don't want to start our new life in the midst of winter, even an Italian winter. I want to start fresh, in early spring, and do everything in the best way possible: proper, unhurried, well thought out, and serendipitous.

◆◆◆◆◆

Friday

13 June 1884

I t's unlucky Friday, the thirteenth, today … and the new "Gravity Pleasure Switchback Railway"—the highest, fastest, and wildest roller coaster yet built—opens for business today on the beach at Coney Island.

Truth be told … I've never ridden a roller coaster before in my entire *life*. I'm thinking that Em and I should ride this railway together—sometime!—before we move to Italy. We should go out "with a bang" so to speak … to go out with some style!

Sunday

15 June 1884

"Real summer" brings real changes for us all.

Baby Lee (also known as Baba), the first grandchild on both sides of the families, is packed off, along with her two nursemaids, to her Lee grandparents to spend the summer with them at Chestnut Hill. Only four months old, Theo and Alice's daughter is already described far and wide as "that cunning, little, yellow-headed Baby Lee." (She's a little beauty, I'll grant you that—yes, I've seen plenty of her on my visits to her surrogate mother, Bamie.)

With the baby away for the summer, Bamie is now free to pay a long, leisurely visit to Aunt Annie and Uncle Jim Gracie at their own Oyster Bay summer house.

Conie finally packs up her own offspring, toddler Teddy Robinson, and returns home to Doug in Orange, New Jersey.

And Theo?

I'm *not* allowed to see him, of course. He still scowls at the mention of my name and warns his sisters to "please let me know in advance when that woman"—*that woman* meaning me—"plans to pay a call on you, and I will most assiduously stay out of your house until she's gone."

But I still hear about him, so that's something. (Yes, I am pathetic enough to *still* devour any stray crumb of news about Theo.)

As soon as he can respectfully leave the Legislature, Theo grabs the first train west to Dakota Territory. I'm also told that, now living in the hinterlands of Medora, Theo purchased his own small herd of cattle—"four hundred head" I believe is the proper terminology.

Bamie continues to fret and wring her hands (and so do I, in secret): "Gosh all hemlock, Edie, he's squandering so much of his inheritance! I only hope he knows what he's *doing*."

So do I. Even the Roosevelt family financial advisor is concerned.

Theo also hired two "cowboys"—about whom he knows very little—named William Merrifield and Sylvane Ferris, to "take care of things" for him at the Maltese Cross Ranch.

Not only *that,* as if one ranch of his own were not enough, now Theo purchased more land to make himself *two* ranches.

Oh, dear heart, have you a nickel left to your name?!

Per Bamie and Connie, Theo's acquisition of the second ranch was purely an impulse purchase. It's deep in the Badlands country of the Little Missouri River ("Little Misery" as local cowboys call it) north of Medora, and Theo aims to call his new ranch the Elkhorn.

So now he needs *more* men to "take care of things" at the Elkhorn Ranch. He's going to import and hire his loyal and trusty old friends—the Maine hunting guides, William Sewall and Sewall's nephew, Wilmot Dow. At the Elkhorn, they'll manage a brand-new, thousand-head herd. That's just for starters.

Theo plans to purchase yet *more* cattle just as soon as he can, even though, according to Bamie, the final bill will probably exceed $80,000.

Such numbers make my head swirl.

I feel physically *sick* with dread.

Meanwhile, my *own* life feels *far* more on an even keel these days. My latest sketches and paintings are much more confident now and less tentative—maybe I could entertain the possibility of an art exhibition sometime? The top drawer of my desk is *stuffed* full of notes about relocating to Italy.

Somehow, somewhere, I feel a most-welcomed cosmic balancing starting to happen.

SATURDAY

29 JUNE 1884

"By the way, Teedie says I should 'stir up the builders, every now and then' in their work on his new house," Bamie informs me today, in a quickly dashed-off letter. (I can tell by her more-careless-than-usual handwriting.) "He also says he is 'collecting heads' to go on the wall. He already has great heaps of them!"

I almost forgot about the new house—dear God.

It's another endless pit of money.

Her letter concludes on a disquieting note: "Poor, dear boy—he probably has no idea that the Republican Party is starting to view him with disfavor. How they loved and pitied him as the new widower this winter and spring, but now ... now that he fled to the Dakotas ... they are starting to view him askance."

I doubt that Theo cares about politics much anymore. His life is all about cows now … all western things. He doesn't care a *fig* about eastern things, except, well, maybe his new house at Oyster Bay.

SUNDAY

27 JULY 1884

Today, I learned—well after the fact—that Theo came back east for a brief summer visit, stopping in at Chestnut Hill, Bamie's Manhattan brownstone, and Republican Party headquarters.

I didn't see him, of course.

I only just heard about Theo's lightning-fast visit from our contract laundress, who happened to mention it to me in passing—after he already left on the train, flanked by his trusty Maine guides, Sewall and Dow.

How much he must do and experience, of which I'll never know about or even guess.

TUESDAY

5 AUGUST 1884

The cornerstone for the Statue of Liberty is laid now on Bedloe's Island in New York Harbor, starting today. I think of the wonderful words of Emma Lazarus that will someday be inscribed along its base.

SATURDAY

10 AUGUST 1884

Early this morning, I felt a shaking and then heard (and felt) a great rumbling—most unnerving indeed!—then, finally it stopped. I thought to myself: *Surely that could not have been an earthquake? Could it? We simply don't have earthquakes in New York state!*

Oh, but we do now!

By this evening's editions of the papers, they all say that it *was*, indeed, a true earthquake: "An earthquake measuring 5.5 Mfa, plus a Mercalli intensity of VII ("very strong") on the Mercalli intensity scale. The earthquake affected a large portion of the eastern United States. Chimneys were toppled throughout New York City, New Jersey, Connecticut, and Pennsylvania. Property damage was severe in some areas."

What's next?!

FRIDAY

15 AUGUST 1884

Conie and I still maintain a brisk correspondence, even though our lives couldn't be more different. Another of her letters shows up today in our mail-slot.

She is the wife of a wealthy, well-connected man and mother of a little boy, all of them living in the lap of luxury. Although she loves her little son, true happiness still seems to elude her. Her husband is dour, her mother-in-law is truly frightening, and she lives so far away from her family and old friends...

...while *I,* the spinster daughter of a penurious widow ... am still waiting, and waiting, and waiting for our Manhattan house (in its sketchy location) to sell so we can start reinventing our lives in sunny Italy.

I wonder...? Am I still unhappy, like Conie? I've been unhappy for *so* very long, I can scarcely remember feeling any other way. But, for the first time in years, I have to say ... no. No, I am *not* unhappy! Although my life isn't perfect just now, new feelings bubble up within me, ripe with good possibilities. It feels so *good* ... not to feel hopeless any longer.

Back to Conie's letter. She still worries about her elder brother. She's worries that he's getting in over his head, as the saying goes. I find my "worry" about him now gradually diminishes with time and distance. I think more about my *own* future these days ... mine and my family's ... instead of Theo's perpetual ups and downs.

I suddenly feel oh-so-*light!* I feel so centered and good.

Conie also writes that Theo keeps asking Sewall and Dow the same question, over and over again, no doubt to subconsciously reassure himself of the rightness of his cattle decisions, a subject about which he still has little practical knowledge: "Don't you think the land around Medora looks like *marvelous* cattle country? It certainly does to me! Doesn't it look that way to you, *too?*"

Sewall and Dow, always polite, yet noncommittal, on this subject, reply that they "like the country well enough, and it certainly is scenic." But they *always* add that it "doesn't look like good cattle country to us, sir, and that's a fact."

Conie includes with her own opinion: "Of course, dear Teedie can still see 'no reason for all this pessimism,' even though Bamie and I certainly can!"

She also writes that the four ranch managers, Westerners Merrifield and Ferris of the Maltese Cross Ranch and Maine guides Sewell and Dow of the soon-to-be-built Elkhorn, walk on eggshells with one another. Merrifield and Ferris got their noses out of joint when Sewall and

Dow first arrived, and Conie writes, "Anyone can see that Teedie prefers the easterners, who displaced Merrifield and Ferris in his esteem."

Oh yes, and one other note: just last week, Theo blithely acquired yet *another* herd of a *thousand cattle*, just arrived from Minnesota. All of his many herds now browse contentedly by the Little Missouri River. I wonder if thinking about all those cattle keep him awake at night?

WEDNESDAY

LATE AUGUST 1884

The specter of Alice arises again in my world. Alice must be "resting uneasy." I tamp down any uncomfortable feelings and put the lid on tightly. I will *not* disturb my newly positive feelings because of anything to do with Alice.

I learn from Bamie and Conie that Theo put together a book of tributes, speeches, newspaper clippings, and letters into a printed memorial about his beloved, late Alice.

Bamie kindly allows me to peruse her copy while I pay a visit to her house yesterday. It will likely be my only opportunity to look at it. I certainly am not on the list of book recipients.

Tonight at home—with the house quiet and everyone in bed but me—I look in the mirror and tell myself (silently): *Stop it! Right* now. *He is not thinking of* you—*hasn't for years—and there's no reason you should think of* him. *Think of Italy, how beautifully your new art pieces are turning out, and the whole new life that awaits you on the Italian Riviera.*

My beloved pup Schatzi looks up at me. Her gaze is mournful. Or is it hopeful? Sometimes, it's hard to tell.

Before turning in for the night, I draw up a letter to our real estate agent, requesting him to reduce the list price of this house … yet again. Yes, I know that, for the most part, our house is on the small side and a bit cramped. Thank goodness for our oversized, elegant front parlor! But *when* will this blasted house ever sell and release the four of us from the bondage of old memories and wasted hopes and dreams?

I pause, then, as if in suspended animation, waiting for an audible answer from … someone? Destiny, perhaps? Or from God?

Schatzi continues to stare at me, fixedly and less mournfully. That will have to suffice in being "my sign." I know that at least *she* will comfort me through yet another lonely night.

As soon as I close the cover of this journal, I will scoop her up and hold her, close to my spinster's heart, and take her right into the bed with me, under the covers and everything—her secret and mine.

SUNDAY

31 AUGUST 1884

I'm currently visiting Conie and Douglas at their seventy-two-acre estate near Orange, New Jersey—and I can't wait to return home again.

It's such a different world here, one in which I don't feel comfortable.

Yes, she and I do some riding—almost every day while the weather is so good. (There's not a great selection of things to *do* in their seventy-two acres of country estate.)

I have a hard time being sociable with them—even with Conie. Her little Teddy is, frankly, a holy terror, forever yelling, smashing china figurines, or sobbing himself into exhausted sleep. And Doug? For someone who is loyal, devoted, generous, and loving to his wife, he is still so personally ... well, irascible. He's so grumpy, touchy, and difficult to love for his own self.

Conie tells me that her beloved brother still broods keenly over Alice's death, confiding that he says, "this pain is beyond any healing for me." I don't know what to think about that—and try not to think of it at all.

In her married life, Conie tends to pace restlessly, not unlike a caged animal. (Yes, true, a gilded cage, but a cage nonetheless.) I know she doesn't love Doug, but she's caught now ... well and truly caught, for good.

I can't wait to board the train for home tomorrow morning.

SATURDAY

20 SEPTEMBER 1884

"One week ago today, a huge grizzly bear reared up not eight paces in front of Teedie, and he shot the bear right between the eyes," Bamie confides in me today from her brother's latest letter. There's more.

"But that's not the strangest thing," says Bamie. "It's what he's *feeling* now that is. Brother writes that he suddenly feels 'oddly purged' … although he doesn't say in what way. Whatever it is, it must be good because he says he's coming back east in three weeks' time to dip his toe in the political process and also to vote in November … I'm thinking he's looking to enter the political arena in a big way!"

Saturday

11 October 1884

Theo is back at Bamie's house on 422 Madison Avenue, telling gangs of newspapermen who clamor outside the front door that he himself is "not a candidate for anything at present."

I'm heartened that Theo appears to be reinventing himself after the agony of losing Alice. But I can't take *too* much joy in that fact because, with an embarrassed yet pitying look, Bamie confides in me today that Theo still "requests that … um … you not visit our house while he's in town, lest he encounter you there, and there'd be a scene, which of course would be distressing to you both—especially to Teedie."

With a polite, frozen visage and in a soft voice, I promise, yet again, to keep myself far from Bamie's house while Theo hangs his hat there, even temporarily.

This is a blow for me. After I've come *so* far in raising my *own* spirits, it is disheartening to hear that Theo still dwells in emotional hades.

He will mourn her forever, and no wonder … after all, she was Alice, the sunshine of his life. She always will be.

MONDAY

13 OCTOBER 1884

Well, the civilized world finally figured *something* out today … both the *Sun* and *New York Tribune* report that the London-based International Meridian Conference "resolved" by twenty-two votes to one (and two abstentions, one of which was France) that Greenwich would be the prime meridian of longitude for our entire world. They explain that a meridian is an imaginary line that passes north to south through the Greenwich Observatory in London, England, dividing the Earth into two equal parts, the Eastern Hemisphere and Western Hemisphere.

What is the point? The prime meridian is at zero degrees longitude, the starting point for the measuring system of longitude all across the globe. It's also the basis for determining the world's time zones. We recently formalized the time zones in America and Canada—now the rest of the world can follow suit.

Monday

27 October 1884

Theo is twenty-six years old today. He's not anywhere in the city where I might "encounter" him, though. He's up in Boston at Henry Cabot Lodge's place, hobnobbing with intellectuals like William Dean Howells, Thomas Bailey Aldrich, and Oliver Wendell Holmes.

To his everlasting credit, Theo has been making speeches on behalf of the worthy, good-hearted Grover Cleveland, even though he's a Democrat. The Republican, Blaine, is so corrupt, he *reeks*. Even someone as apolitical as myself can see that.

THURSDAY

6 NOVEMBER 1884

Three days ago, Grover Cleveland became our twenty-second president ... the first Democrat in twenty-five years. Judging by what little I know of it, I like him. I know Theo does, too.

I hear by the grapevine that Theo is taking the first train today, heading west back to the Dakota Territory.

I'm still frequently stopping in at the Consulate General of Italy in New York City, making notes and getting the necessary information for Americans intending to relocate abroad. I also met three times with Cruikshank and Sons—and will do so again—to sort out exactly how, when, and where we can best manage and access our American funds in Italy (which will be ample enough once we sell the dratted house! ... certainly enough to pay monthly rent and keep food on the table). I also check with steamship companies to compare prices and timetables of travel from NYC to Liverpool and then on to London.

Theo isn't the *only* one planning a new life, you know! Two can play that game.

S omething *huge* happened today. Jack Traynor Stratton came back into my life— only … I couldn't do anything about it. I literally *ran into* Jack today. He was buying a paper from the corner news agent, and he looked up just as I approached him. He smiled with incredulous delight. His clothes were far less dapper than I remembered, but he looked happier and somehow more "well fed."

"Jack! You're *back!*" I cry, clutching at his arm (and not intending to create a little rhyme). My mind whirls with unspoken words: *Why didn't you come straightaway to see me? Why didn't you let me know you returned to the city? WHY?* "The fact that you're back must mean … what was it? At least six hundred thousand Adirondack acres were pulled back into state lands for nonpayment of back taxes? Your crusade to save the area was a smashing success?"

"Yes!" he exclaims with delight. "That's *exactly* what it means!" He squeezes my hand in both of his. "Oh, it is *so* good to see you again!" (He looked like he meant it, too. He seemed very happy and excited, yet simultaneously wistful, sheepish, and sad.)

He rattles on: "The tax thing happened at the end of last year, *finally* … thank goodness! The state of New York now controls the land in question and will not let it go again! Already they're taking legal steps to make the Adirondacks a New York State Park, preserving it in perpetuity. Who knows? Maybe the federal government will start protecting places too, someday. When it does, I'll make sure the Adirondacks get in at the head of the line for federal protection."

We both laugh in agreement—*and* happiness that a such positive happenstance thing *can* happen in this world, not just always bad news.

"As you might guess, a lot happened to me since I went to the North Woods…" Jack starts fingering the perimeter of his well-worn "boater" straw hat brim, nervously.

I try to keep the conversation cheerful. "That's a bit of an understatement! It looks like a *lot* happened to you!" Then, I stop smiling so wide.

My smile becomes a bit tremulous, and I can't help but ask, "But why did you not come to see me? I *did* get your long letter explaining the rift with your father and uncles and about why you opted to stay and fight for the land that you loved. I sent you back a letter that was *equally* long! Did you not receive it?"

I try not to sound pathetic—just "interested."

"No, I never received that letter." He looks somber at that moment but keeps on fiddling with his hat brim. Nerves…

Then, Jack reluctantly extends his left hand toward me. I could see a silver wedding band on the fourth finger of his left hand. He speaks softly and a bit haltingly, too. "Like I said, a lot of things changed for me up north. I had to get used to being poor, for one thing!" (He laughed, and I couldn't help but smile along with him.) "I never received your long letter. I wish I had … But by then, I'd already met Charlotte, who was also on the committee to save the land. We were much thrown together in our mutual work, and it was only inevitable that our friendship should turn to … well, you know!"

"How … how long have you two been married?" I am still so shocked—I don't know why … it's such a natural thing to have happened.

"These past six months," he replies.

"Charlotte! Tell me a little about Charlotte." I really don't know what to say, but I am curious about the girl who put a ring on Jack's finger.

"She teaches the lower grades at the Saranac Lake school. Once she finishes out this term, she'll be giving her notice, though. The school board doesn't like to see married women taking a job that a man might need to feed his family."

The skewed logic of that turned my stomach sour. I say nothing about that, but I do ask, "So are you coming back to the city then, to live with Charlotte?"

He smiles a bit ruefully. "No, I'm just here in the city for a few meetings and then on to Albany to meet with legislators who might be able to help our cause."

"And Charlotte is…?"

He shakes his head imperceptibly. "No, she's back in Saranac, teaching. I'll be heading back in a week or so."

"So Charlotte sounds like she must be a very accomplished and educated young lady … or young matron, I should say. Does she like the theater … too?" I laugh a little, trying to make a joke of it. Jack and I always *loved* the theater! We were *so* lucky that way, having some of the best theater in the world at our feet, as it were.

"I'm sure Charlotte would love the theater if she could, but you know we have very little in the way of entertainment in the north woods. There are beautiful lakes and mountains but no … Broadway theater." He sounds a little unhappy about that, but we both smile and nod.

Then Jack quits fiddling with his hat, places it atop his head, and adjusts it with a tug. "Well, I'd best be going. I'm to meet with a committee member here shortly."

I am surprised when he pulls me in for a quick but very close hug. (I remembered how it felt that time when the buttons of his overcoat pressed into my front, all the way down.)

"Don't be such a stranger now!" I smile at him in farewell. "You know where I live!" (For *now*, I was thinking, but not long from now, I'll be living in Italy, and you will forever lose track of me, but that will be all for the best.)

I also tell Jack that we would always, *always* be good friends. Thus my last bridge is burned today … without any action on my part.

I am now ready to lead the spinster's life.

I will always serve as the main support of my family of misfit women—lugubrious, hypochondriac Mamma; annoying, gangly Em; and dear, loyal, aging Mame. At least I won't be *alone* in this life—I know (and sometimes worry) that I will *always* have the care and feeding of these three as my first responsibility. Maybe things *will* be different for me—for my family—in Italy. We'll bask in so much sunshine! I'll paint wonderful new scenes of the Mediterranean coast, olive groves, and fields of red poppies. I'll lead my own life, a *new* life— one that is not connected in *any* way to one Roosevelt in particular. That suits me just fine.

New Year's Eve

31 December 1884

Am I feeling remorse? Second thoughts? Maybe.

Maybe it's because the house *still* hasn't sold.

Maybe I'm just so unutterably tired.

Maybe I've simply lost hope, in everyone and everything.

Doctors these days are starting to talk about a new phenomenon they call mental depression or, more commonly, melancholia. I'm pretty sure I have a textbook case of it.

Although I still occasionally perform good deeds to get myself out of the house (and keep my family from worrying about my mental state), I've cut back on my duties. I plan to cut back even more in the new year. I still paint and sketch, but not so much these days. It's hard to even get motivated.

I envision my future self staying around home more, keeping Mamma company, reading worthy books, and perhaps becoming a literary-loving recluse like Emily Dickinson. Who would care either way? I'm past caring.

I can't be bothered to make journal entries anymore. What's the point? What's the use?

I'm locking this book away in my treasure box. There it shall stay—forever, if need be, until such time as something stirs me from my doldrums and sets me back on the road to life.

WEDNESDAY

17 JUNE 1885

I just had to break my silence to record this: the Statue of Liberty arrived in New York Harbor today! That's *certainly* a worthy impetus to make me write in this diary again!

The statue's long voyage was on the French frigate *Isere*, and the Lady Liberty actually came in two hundred and fourteen *crates* that held the disassembled gift from the People of France. Nearly a quarter of a *million* people lined Battery Park to watch the spectacle, while hundreds of boats pulled into the harbor to welcome the *Isere*.

I'm glad to hear that plenty-enough money was raised to make a pedestal for the Lady, and now I know that the inspiring sonnet by Emma Lazarus, "Give me your tired, your poor, your huddled masses yearning to breathe free," will live forever inscribed on the pedestal's brass plaque.

Recently, I inquired whether Emma Lazarus will have any more public poetry readings in the near future, but I hear that she is ill ... perhaps quite gravely ill. Nonetheless, she is still heading out on her second trip to Europe, perhaps to grasp more of life while she still can...

MONDAY

22 JUNE 1885

Dear old Woman's Journal, how thrilled you must be to see the light of day again! Especially after being locked in darkness for, lo, these past six months.

Yes, something finally "enchanted me back into life" ... well, at least prompting me to make journal entries again.

I feel like I'm awakening from a dream and more alive now than I've been in months, thanks in great part to Aunt Annie. What is this impetus ... this catalyst ... this irresistible object that calls me back to life?

It's none other than a house—Leeholm.

Yes, *that* house. *Her* house.

Alice's house. (But yet *not* Alice's house, not anymore.)

Let me explain.

Ever my champion and "savior of my sanity," Aunt Annie Gracie recently refused to take no for my reply to her invitation. "Of *course,* you're coming to visit me at Gracewood, you silly girl! I'm wild to show off my new summer house, and such a dear little house it is. You can't help but love it. Let's go out on the train together this Saturday and stay for a week. Bamie's out there, too, already staying at Leeholm, getting it all polished and ready for its master to come and see it in its new glory. He's coming out next week for a five-week holiday, and we shall see *lots* of Theo's house besides my own place. It's just a five-minute walk through the woods from Gracewood."

I say yes automatically. How could I do otherwise to my favorite honorary aunt? So here I am, finally, blissfully ensconced at Aunt Annie's charming summer home, Gracewood—and it's utterly perfect. I drink in new air for a change, clean and bracing, with a faint tang of salt, not the over-used, fusty air of the city.

After breakfast on the porch with Aunt Annie, and after praising the exquisite appointments of Gracewood, I feel my heart lurch with excitement when she casually suggests, "Why don't you head on over to Leeholm while I finish up some correspondence? It's just a step through the woods, and I'll catch you up shortly."

I'm not about to be asked twice.

I try to walk sedately, following the trail through velvet-green woods, lush with life renewing itself.

Then, I find myself breaking into a run.

There, at the edge of the woods, a vast wheatfield begins ... and it's there that the house has taken root.

Leeholm.

There are no architectural pretentions to Leeholm, though it's good-sized and sprawling. It seems to exude a sense of coziness. It's oddly welcoming and, yes, homey.

Although the shingled siding is painted a sickly mustard color ... (whose idea was *that,* I wonder) ... the dark-green trim suits it.

A broad, covered veranda graces the south and west sides of the house. To the north and west, the lawn slopes down.

I can see Oyster Bay in the distance, sparkling with sun glints. I can even see the faraway Connecticut shore.

For a little while, I hang back, observing a gardening crew—undoubtedly hired and supervised by Bamie, preparing for Theo's upcoming visit—as they plant vines, shrubs, saplings, and flowers.

A slender but already handsome copper beech tree is planted close to the house. (How I've always admired a lovely copper beech.)

Finally, I approach the house and call out a greeting to Bamie, just as Aunt Annie joins me. (Good timing on my part.)

Bamie brings fresh tea out to the veranda. We three pull new rocking chairs conspiratorially together.

Bless their hearts, Aunt Annie and Bamie chatter endlessly about Theo, Elliott, and Conie. I lap up the gossip with barely disguised interest.

Without divulging any of my own secrets, I learn that while my winter of 1884–85 was that of a contemplative nun, Theo's days and nights were crammed with experiences, adventures, and literary determination.

Yes, he wrote another book! *Hunting Trips of a Ranchman* was created while he resided in his guest bedroom at Bamie's Madison Avenue brownstone. He'd come there for Christmas but then decided to stay for two full months to finish his new book.

On 8 March 1885, he finally finished the book and whisked it off to the publisher. But the book project left Theo utterly drained, as well as physically and emotionally fragile.

"Sister and I are *horribly* nervous about all this ... this latest venture of Theo's. We keep wondering, what *can* he be doing with dear Father's patrimony? His money keeps going out, and out, and out, and thus far, nothing much is coming back in."

I don't think Bamie intends to divulge so much, but words pour from her as if from an auctioneer. "You *know* I keep asking Theo for guarantees that this 'cattle project' will eventually pay off—and pay big. But all Theo will say is, 'I can't guarantee it, Sister, but I honestly *believe* that it will. Eventually.' *Honestly*."

She repeats the word with a scoff: "Eventually!"

I concur one hundred percent with Bamie on this, but it isn't my place to comment on their brother's business acumen. I say nothing, but I make some appropriately polite sounds of empathy.

Aunt Annie chimes in with her own worries for her eldest nephew. "Did you know when Teedie took the train back to Dakota in mid-April, he was in such a weakened state the he literally had to be helped aboard the train? Thin as a reed, he was, so tired and pale. We were all frightened to death about him, and we begged Conie's husband to correspond with the Maine guides, explaining that his women back east are all worried about him, requiring periodic reports about his health."

He must not be in *too* bad shape now because I learned that Theo took the Maine guides Sewall and Dow along with him, plus Mr. Ferris, to help Mr. Merrifield bring back yet *another* fifteen hundred head of cattle. This latest purchase amounted to $39,000—a shocking, unthinkable sum, more than half of his remaining inheritance. He wrote that they had a deuce of a time driving the cattle all the way from Minnesota to the Maltese Cross Ranch, plagued by stampedes, thirsty cattle driven close to madness, dust, exhaustion, and more.

In mid-May, a pale and thin Theo showed up to assist with the annual Badlands spring round-up. He often stayed up all night on watch and returned to work—roping steers until his hands were raw—after a quick 3 a.m. breakfast.

During the five-week round-up, more than sixty men riding three hundred horses coaxed four thousand cattle out of the creeks, coulees, basins, ravines, and gorges, sorting them into proprietary herds and branding every calf with the mark of its mother. Theo finally wrapped it up—just days ago—to catch the eastbound train for New York. Then something else happened. Something Good.

Just this morning, Bamie's latest letter from Theo (which she passed around to the rest of us) seems uncharacteristically cheerful and redolent with … what feels like hope.

He writes that "something strange but good recently happened to me."

I only *wish* that I could stick around for his visit and find out what this good thing is.

Sorry, Miss Carow. It's not possible.

VERY LATE AT NIGHT … AND I'M OH, SO TIRED.

SATURDAY

4 JULY 1885

Theo's latest book, *Hunting Trips of a Ranchman*, was finally released by G.P. Putnam's Sons on 1 July.

The book's dedication read, "To that keenest of sportsmen and truest of friends, my brother, Elliott Roosevelt."

I managed to purchase a copy for myself, even though it was wickedly expensive—enough for a new dress and pair of shoes besides.

Yet many working people lined up to buy this very elegant book with its thick, creamy, hand-woven paper and sumptuous engravings.

It also features a frontispiece photo of Theo in his buckskins and moccasins, taken in front of a false background of flowers and ferns. It's odd but so endearing, at least to me.

I stayed up late last night reading it. It's superb—only what I'd expect from any book of Theo's.

Earlier tonight, I took Em and Mame to see the Fourth of July fireworks at Riverside Park—we splurged on a hansom cab both ways. Mamma decided to stay home with a cold cloth on her forehead (much better that way).

Tonight, amid the throngs and throughout each red and blue explosion of man-made stars, my mind is far away … ruminating on yesterday's letter from Conie.

Conie writes, "Something happened to my elder brother recently—a metamorphosis in body and spirit. I don't know how or why. *He* won't say, of course! He came to our house in Orange recently, and you'd never know him. I scarcely knew him *myself!* An article in the *Times* recently described him as 'rugged, bronzed, and in the prime of health.' They certainly got *that* right! He must have put on thirty pounds! Another reporter—this one from the *Post*—writes that he is 'struck by Mr. Roosevelt's sturdy walk and firm bearing.' Even that Maine guide, Mr. Sewall, writes to us that Theo is 'as husky as any man I have ever seen who wasn't dependent on his arms for his livelihood.' When I asked Theo about his asthma and the dreaded cholera morbus, he just smiled and said, 'Oh, they've disappeared.' And he's decided the name for the house must be changed. No more Leeholm. Instead, the house will bear the name of an old Indian 'Sagamore,' which Brother says is an Indian word for 'chieftain.' Theo's going to call the house Sagamore Hill."

FRIDAY

17 JULY 1885

I hear through the grapevine that Theo invited Fanny Smith Dana to his first house party up at Sagamore Hill.

Wouldn't you just know it.

Fanny is now married to her naval man. I didn't attend her wedding because it was in Annapolis—too expensive to travel there. Her husband is called Commander Dana; he's very handsome with hair as dark as Fanny's.

Then, I hear through that same grapevine that Fanny is slowly recovering from a miscarriage, and suddenly, I feel ashamed of mean-spirited thoughts.

Still, I can't stop wondering if they're ever going to "catch" one another between spouses … she and Theo, I mean. She's always been mad for him; any fool could see that. Fanny would make an *adoring* wife for him. She radiates happiness at everything and anything Theo ever says or does, even if it's ill-advised or silly.

Now I, well…

I may not be the wife he would choose to make him happy, obviously, but I know that I could—and *would*—bring out the highest and best in Theo. I would bring out his greatness. I just *know* I would.

But that's neither here nor there. Remember, Italy awaits me—eventually. Remember that and stay steadfast.

LATE NIGHT ON SATURDAY
8 AUGUST 1885

Earlier this week, Bamie wrote me: "The whole family is coming back into the city for General Grant's funeral parade. Theo is going to march as a captain in the National Guard."

But, today, I don't get to see Theo march, nor see the expression on his face as he passes by with his regiment, crepe floating from his rifle.

Something else, more momentous, takes center stage: suddenly, our house is *sold*.
Italy, here I come!

Here's how it happens. A furniture manufacturer of modest means, a Mr. Ephraim and his wife, seek to relocate their small company from upstate New York to the "better prospects" of the big city. They seek "suitable quarters" in our general neighborhood, and they think our house will do for them just fine.

Our house is finally under contract. Sold! At *last*.

It's taken so long I can scarcely believe it. But it's finally *true*.

Though the price they offer is far from what I originally wanted, still, it's respectable and will get us where we want (and need) to go. We can work with it.

Over the telephone, our real estate agent urges Mamma (and me) to "take the offer, *please*, Mrs. Carow. You'll never get a better amount in today's market."

I rapidly add the numbers up in my head. Even after paying off our mortgage and sundry small loans, there will still be a tidy sum for steamship tickets, moving expenses, and initial rent at a pensione on the Italian coast. There's even money left over for visiting Mamma's cousins while in England.

Mamma looks up at me from the telephone speaker, and I nod.

Sold.

The buyers can't make the actual move until May 1886, but we'll pay monthly rent to them (instead of mortgage money to the bank) until we make the switch. All the better for us. We don't want to move to Italy—let alone spend time in England—in the dead of winter. Quickly, I think it all out; we'll leave in April 1886.

Suddenly, I shiver. Our lives will never be the same again.

But that's *all right,* that's *good,* that's *as it should be,* I remind myself, trying to ignore unnamed pangs, yearnings, and heartache.

I'll reinvent myself in Italy. You'll see … it will be all right. It *will.*

Thursday

3 September 1885

What's *happening* to our world these days? To the United States I thought I knew and loved? How can such barbaric things happen here? Yesterday in Rock Springs, Wyoming Territory, one hundred and fifty white miners attacked Chinese railroad workers—the people who do most of the dirty work on the rails. The white miners murdered twenty-eight Chinese, wounded fifteen more, and forced several hundred others to "get your miserable yellow selves" out of town.

I pray that Italy will afford us a kinder and more inspiring place in which to live.

Tuesday

6 October 1885

Destiny can be funny sometimes. *What a pitiful way to describe it! Let me try again.*

Destiny is a rocket, exploding overhead, raining down on you with stars that burn.

Destiny is a bolt from the blue, knocking you forever off balance.

Destiny can turn your knees to gelatin and your ankles to rubber, even as it ignites your heart on fire.

Even as it ignites my *own* heart today.

I'm going to write it all down ... bit by bit ... exactly as it happened, minute by minute. That's the only way I can read it and reread it ... and read it yet again, to start to believe that destiny's appearance in my life is really *real* this time.

I'll begin.

I'm here at 422 Madison Avenue, visiting Bamie at her stylish new home. Baby Lee pitches an untimely, royal *fit*.

Theo's golden-haired daughter is nearly two years old now, her Auntie Bamie's pride and joy—and utter exasperation, too.

I always think: *Thank goodness for Baby Lee's nursemaid and Bamie's other servants to do the endless washing of diapers and picking up messes left in the toddler's wake, without which there would never be any "time alone" for oneself, ever.* (For numerous reasons, Bamie is truly blessed by her wealth, but having constant help in caring for Baby Lee is certainly at the top of her list, in my humble opinion)

Bamie and I are supposed to step out together today to explore ("to snoop!" as I call it) at Casters & Company, a new antique and furnishings shop. But Baby Lee now turns herself into a noodle, falling to the floor and kicking her heels on the hearth rug as she screams and cries. "Me wanna go *too!* Wanna go, wanna *go!*"

Exhausted yet obdurate, Bamie shakes her head. "No, dearie. No. It's time for *you* to take a much-needed *nap*, especially with your Papa coming home tomorrow on the train."

(I see Theo is already headed back to spend the autumn and winter in the east. I wonder what he would say about his daughter's growing tantrum if he were here to witness it.)

Baby Lee screams like a steam engine. She scarcely draws breath between words. "No! *No!!* Wanna go, *me* wanna go too!"

Bamie looks at me in confused defeat—what to do? We can't possibly take Baby Lee with us to Casters & Company.

I can't help laughing at the little blonde wretch, wrapping her doting auntie around her sticky fingers.

"Never mind," I reassure Bamie. "We'll explore Casters another time. I can see you've got your hands full here!"

My smile turns wry as Baby Lee flings herself from side to side in a fit of thwarted pride and anger. Helplessly, the nursemaid tries to pull her up by her arms, but Baby Lee becomes more noodle-like than ever.

Bamie sinks into an overstuffed chair—at her wit's end.

I lean down to give Bamie a brief, one-armed hug. "It's all right. Don't get up. I'll see myself out."

Bamie is relieved to agree. "Another time, then! Thanks for understanding, Edie."

I nod and wave in assent, exit the upstairs nursery, walk to the end of the hall, and start down the stairs between the second and first floors, when…

(But I'm getting ahead of myself here. I must go back a bit.)

Meanwhile, around this same time, a man—a stocky Westerner with a handlebar mustache—steps off the train here in the city. How pleased (and surprised!) his family will be to see that he's taken the train a full day earlier than planned.

He directs a hansom cab to take him to 422 Madison Avenue. The cabbie directs his horse to halt the rig in front of the house. The cabbie deposits a couple of valises by the front door. The Westerner pays and tips the cabbie, pulls his own front door key from his coat pocket, and quietly unlocks the front door.

He aims to surprise them all.

After opening the door, he peers around for servants or any other signs of life. No servants are in evidence—*good*. He can make his way around stealthily and give his family a good-natured fright. First, what *is* that ungodly noise? He isn't sure.

(It's Baby Lee, with her piercing voice rising to a crescendo of utter rage, sounding more like a whistling tea kettle than anything else—not exactly human at the moment.)

The Westerner heads for the stairs to the second floor…

…just as a feminine figure in sensible dark blue serge (the spinster Miss Carow) starts descending the steps.

At the very same time, we see each other … Theo and I.

It's been almost two years.

We both freeze—momentarily—in our steps.

I tremble as shimmering electricity fills my body. (I don't know what Theo feels.) I can't worry about that—I must rise to this occasion with grace and dignity.

I struggle to regain my composure and slowly complete my descent of the stairs like a graceful sleepwalker. I still retain enough presence of mind to remember a piece of very good advice: "A man sees a woman at her *very* best when she descends a staircase."

I try (somehow) to look especially "alluring," even dressed as I am in my blue, serge walking suit. Thank goodness I'm wearing my attractive new gaucho hat!

Slowly, I step down to where he stands, evidently rooted to the floor.

Upstairs, two muffled, protesting female voices are no match for Baby Lee's continuing outburst. She has only gotten started.

We pay no mind to the noise from upstairs. We have more important things going on here between us.

As I descend the last step, we are almost toe to toe.

So close…

I look up at Theo from under the brim of my plumed gaucho hat. For once in my life, I'm wearing the latest style in hats. I know my "fold-less" eyes are at their blue-gray best when framed by the so-called lunatic fringe—these curled bangs are all the rage now.

Finally, he speaks.

His voice is soft and low, uncharacteristically deep yet touched with uncertainty. "I've been wondering what I would say to you if we … uh … ever saw one another again."

"That will do as well as anything," I reply softly, with a faint Mona Lisa smile.

I try hard to quell my astonishment, surprise, and admiration. *He looks so different now, much stockier. I would hardly know him if I saw him on the street—but, of course, I do know him … would always know him, anywhere…*

We continue to stand there, and dozens of emotions flicker across his face.

I watch, fascinated.

I realize … no, I *know* … that Theo knows about me—about it *all*.

Conie, Bamie, Elliott, Aunt Annie, or his cousins—someone, *everyone*, must have tattled to Theo about the gradual decline in the Carow family income, the death of my poor Papa, and how the Carow women now have to rummage about, seeking additional means of support so our eroded annuity can support us more fully.

Suddenly, I feel as if I'm made of glass—naked—with no way to prevent him from seeing those many elements about which I'm embarrassed or ashamed—not marrying another man for money or my "utter non-susceptibility" to other men, period. *Why* did I wear such a "sensible" (ugly) gown today? Ugh. I must look every inch the aging old maid that I am. At least my gaucho hat, with its white plume curling sideways across my bangs, shows that I'm still trying to be a woman—a poor yet determined woman, trying hard to remain attractive, and desirable, despite my limited resources.

The silence grows longer between us, painfully so.

But we can't help but stare at each other while Baby Lee shrieks upstairs, punctuated by soothing yet ineffectual sounds from Bamie and the nursemaid.

Theo looks so different now, it's shocking to me. He looks *nothing* like Alice Lee's widower *(thank goodness)*. He's brown as an Indian Rajah, bulging arms not quite hidden by his coat (muscles, surely?). His bull neck is thick, framed by bulky shoulders. His drooping, reddish-brown mustache spells "cowboy."

At least I can see his lower lip is still beautiful, and I'm assuming his mustache-hidden upper lip is just as beautiful, too.

He takes off his hat. It's dark gray, broad-rimmed, flat topped, and thoroughly Western. His hair still grows out in waves, but now it's sun gilded and cropped shorter than I've ever seen it.

His eyes are still big and blue behind his glasses.

I stand, motionless and preternaturally calm, against his scrutiny. What does he see when he looks at me?

He probably sees a small-waisted, not very tall spinster with a figure like the number eight. I don't need to sew rows of ruffles into my corset cover to achieve the desired effect.

He probably notices that my hands and feet are still small and ladylike—not yet careworn by time and circumstance.

My widely spaced gray eyes still have no folds. They look like the eyes of a surprised girl from across the western sea, one with thick, straight, dark (almost unfeminine) eyebrows. I know this is not a "look" that's currently in fashion—a demerit in my small arsenal of charms.

I think of my lips and suddenly feel better.

I'm glad our own lips are still so much alike. Both of us have upper and lower lips that are equal in size, mirror images of each other.

My skin is yet unlined—it's got a pale-pink tint. My nose is long and narrow, like an ancient Greek statue.

My breathing speeds up, and my face slowly turns scarlet. Suddenly, I can scarcely catch my breath at all.

The wails of Baby Lee continue upstairs, but they seem to lose steam.

We have to do something fast. *Now*, before the moment is lost.

He quickly glances up the stairs and then back at me. "May I meet you again … privately?"

"Yes," I whisper, still maintaining my Mona Lisa smile. I don't seem to be able to speak the words any louder, for some reason.

I add, "I like your Western mustache … it suits you."

He says nothing about the mustache. He seems concerned and urgent about something else.

"First thing tomorrow morning?" he asks in a low voice, wanting an answer before our … situation … is discovered.

My Mona Lisa smile softens my face. "Yes."

Again I whisper, even more softly.

"Meet me at the sailboat slips at Riverside Park … you remember where the—?"

I interrupt him with another whisper. "Yes."

Another smile blooms on my face, and this time I can feel my teeth showing. I bless my good fortune that they're still pretty and still white.

"Nine o'clock, then. At the signpost by the sailboat slips." He still sounds uncertain, wanting to hear my corroboration before we part today.

With intent clearly on my face and a thrill stirring my heart, I answer him: "Nine o'clock."

He nods. Briefly, he touches my hand with his.

The touch almost makes me fly out of my skin, but I say nothing. I just nod back at him.

Then, he steps past me and starts marching up the stairs toward the sounds of Baby Lee, Bamie, and the nursemaid.

I turn away, too, and head for the front door. But I can't help looking back over my shoulder to see him—one more time—and I see that he is looking back at me, too, just for a moment. He reaches the top of the staircase, moves toward the nursery, and flings open the door. I hear peals of happy laughter and surprised greetings from within.

I exit, close the door behind me, and leave Bamie's house with speed.

Nobody has seen us. Nobody knows.

Nobody knows that my life is about to change—yet again.

Hang on, dear Journal—I'm going to mix some metaphors. A lot of them!

For starters, the opaque onion-skins of my late teens and early twenties are suddenly ripped off my eyes—and my heart. After many months, no, *years,* I can fully *see* things as they really are again. I can feel again, love again.

With no forethought or foreboding, I fling myself into the sea of love. Its waters are dangerous, deep, and irresistible.

Loving Theo is an all-or-nothing proposition for me. My love for him is as boundless as the sea, and I don't care if I drown in it with him.

These last few days … *I can't begin to even tell you.*

It's impossible to recreate our early, furtive meetings on these flat pages. Theo is too big, too bold, too boisterous ... too brimming with unaccounted-for happiness, heartening to see in him after years of grief.

This positive new feeling surprises him. It baffles, annoys, and disturbs him *greatly*. Nonetheless, each time we conclude our brief rendezvous, he asks me, sotto voce: "Can we meet again privately? And ... soon?"

Monday

12 October 1885

I finally convince Theo, "We've *got* to stop these 'secret assignations' ... both for your sake *and* for mine."

What may sound like meetings in a secret love-nest are anything *but* that for Theo and me. No, we remain circumspect, upright citizens—worse luck. Instead, we meet in the Shakespeare section of the Astor Library, at an out-of-the-way tea room on a narrow street, and in Riverside Park under our favorite linden tree, now golden and shedding its leaves—this tree is well secluded from passersby.

I caution him: "Someone is bound to find out and try to ruin you with this politically." It's true. I worry about this all the time.

He shoots me a look, sober and quizzical. *(So you no longer wish to meet with me privately, then?)*

I gaze steadily back at him. *(Not so fast, Mr. Roosevelt!)* My heart thuds so loudly in my chest, he must be able to hear it. The gaze I radiate back to him should leave no doubt as to the depth and extent of my feelings.

"Theodore…" In a soft voice, I use his given name. He looks surprised and (almost?) pleased. "We must, both of us, come out into 'the light of day' as…"

I *hate* to say it because I don't mean it at *all.* But it's the right thing to say. It's the right thing to do.

"As long-time family friends."

Instantly, he agrees. "You're right, you're right, of course! People might get … ideas. So here's what we'll do. We'll nonchalantly inform family and friends that we just happened to run into one another, right out here on the street! We'll tell everyone that we finally buried the hatchet."

He looks at me under lowered brows. "Uh … we have, haven't we? Buried the hatchet?"

I roll my eyes at him with emotion I can't hide and rebuke him in mock severity. "If you have to ask about *that*…"

So that's just what we do, Theo and I.

As Theo tells me soon after, "So, during family dinner the other night with Uncle Jimmie, I 'just happened to mention' to Bamie, and also to Conie and Doug, who were visiting, 'Guess who I ran into the other day? Edith Carow!' Of course, everybody exclaimed and looked concerned, knowing of our … previous estrangement. But I assured everyone, 'No, no … it's all fine and set to rights again. Bygones are bygones, and Edie and I are back to being our same old chums again.' And do you know what Conie said to this? 'Well, it *took* you long enough'!"

We both had a good laugh at that, while inwardly I had to agree with Conie.

How many years it has taken you to give me another chance?

I used pretty much the same play script with my family. Mamma grumbled a little—she still thinks all Roosevelts are diseased—but she took our reconciliation (Theo's and mine) as an event of minor note, while Em and Mame shot me knowing looks. Em may be twitchy, talky, and nervous, but she's nobody's fool about my romantic life. Mame may be showing her age, but she's still unfailingly perceptive.

I don't elaborate my story to them. I only say it'll be "nice to do things with the Roosevelts again without tiptoeing around on eggshells all the time." It is true. Finally—eventually—they drop the subject and move on to another topic.

We still talk about Italy. Italy *is* going to happen for me and my family—no matter what happens with Theo. (I refuse to even think of this at all—too many complications.)

Finally, our families and friends start treating the reconciliation of Teedie and Edie as old news. They move on to the next tidbit of gossip as, meanwhile, Theo invites me as his "special houseguest" to Sagamore Hill for his twenty-seventh birthday party, coming up in just sixteen days.

I now move blithely through the days, careful to play the role of long-time platonic playmate from years gone by. No one is the wiser, maybe even Theo, because … dear Lord, I really can't tell *what* he thinks.

Oh, he's very fond and happy, but still, he hasn't kissed me yet or even given me a hug.

I lie awake for much of each night, wondering and worrying.

Does he still mourn Alice?

Will he *always* mourn her?

Am I living in a fool's paradise to even consider things might change in my favor regarding him? What about my new life in Italy? It's a paradise place where I could set myself up as an artist, with new adventures, new horizons to explore? What about *that?*

At least Theo's sterling reputation for propriety, decorum, and morality remains unsullied among New York's high society. Thank goodness…

But the official period of mourning … it hasn't been *near* long enough.

Alice has been gone only eighteen months. Society requires at least five years of decorous mourning for a departed wife.

A shocking scandal would explode across New York society if Theo were to start courting me—publicly—now.

I don't want anything to sully Theo's name, politically or personally. Not ever. It shouldn't, for he's done nothing "amiss" with me—yet.

But will he ever … someday?

I wonder: Did he reconcile with me only to make *his* life "flow more smoothly?"

I'll find out at my upcoming visit to Sagamore Hill, not as a nosy neighbor but *this* time as a full-fledged invited guest.

It's about time.

MONDAY

27 OCTOBER 1885

No, make that 2 a.m. on 28 October—T's twenty-seventh birthday.

As self-contained and solitary as I was *before* Theo came back into my life, that's how bursting with life and joy I am *now* … now that he's back, pulling me into the mainstream of life with him, whether I like it or not. I *do* like it. I crave his presence like air and sunshine.

Yes, Italy *is* waiting in the wings for me. I must do it. My family is counting on me.

Although craving Theo's proximity, I still manage to turn my lovesickness into relaxed laughter, nonchalance, and jokes. I keep up the platonic "old family friend" façade with surprising ease. (Perhaps I should become an actress, instead of a prim spinster—you know how I adore the theater!)

No one—well, maybe except for servants (especially Mame) and sisters (especially Em)—suspects a thing.

For Theo's birthday party and house party guests, he decided to host—and try for the first time himself—a sport he's never before attempted: fox hunting with hounds. His friend Henry Cabot Lodge insists, "Just try it. You'll love it! Just wait and see."

Theo will be wearing the traditional pink coat and "hardened" hat, all the usual regalia.

Conie and I planned to join the riders, despite the rough terrain ahead—that is, until I heard that Long Island's Meadowbrook Hunt Club was running the event. "We'll be tackling some of the toughest fields in the world!" Lodge confides to me, almost salivating with anticipation.

Conie and I are no strangers to a sidesaddle and riding crop, but not this—so much competition by "professionals." It's all too much. We happily opt to sit this one out; we'll hear about it after the fact.

As the hunt finally concludes and riders return to the barn—some of them much the worse for wear—I finally demand (and receive) a full report from Henry Cabot Lodge. I can't really ask Theo yet because, despite his grin and high spirits, *he* is the bloodiest of them all!

According to Lodge, Theo "gallops after the fox with the same fierce energy and flashing, toothsome grin as if he were hunting bison." Yes, the country is very rough—yes, the timbered obstacles stand more than five feet high, one right after another, six to every mile. It's *very* dangerous. (I'm so glad I didn't go—I would have killed myself, so out of practice am I with anything to do with horses these days.)

Riding a rambunctious stallion, Theo leads the pack. Riders fall right and left, but most of them remount and forge ahead, despite the mud and blood. Even Conie's husband Doug takes a nasty spill and peels some of the skin right off his face.

Then, Theo's horse trips going over a wall. Both horse and rider pitch into a pile of rocks.

Theo's face smashes up against something sharp, drawing much blood. His left arm—only recently beginning to heal after a fracture during the last cattle roundup—snaps just beneath the elbow.

Here's Lodge in his own words: "So, like a crazed savage, he gets back in the saddle as soon as the horse is up and starts galloping off again. Meanwhile, his useless left arm just dangles from his shoulder. Blood is still *pouring* down his face, but still, even thus, he keeps on galloping across fifteen—yes, fifteen!—more fields. He finally finishes the hunt within a hundred yards of the other riders, looking like the walls of a slaughterhouse when he gets back to the stables."

I know, I *know*—I see *this* part of the story in person as I and others wait by the stables to hear what happened on the chase. Even Baby Lee, who's here waiting with her nurse, runs away screaming at the bloody monster who is her father, even as Theo runs after her with pretend growls and laughter.

Finally, bathed and dressed in his dancing clothes, his arm in splints and a sling, his cut face plastered and bandaged, he presides over the Hunt Ball with confidence and ease, as if he's the laird of Sagamore himself.

All day and all night, Theo seems so … happy and somehow surprised by it.

We manage to get in three dances together—the absolute limit before "people will talk"—and then it's time for guests to sing "For He's a Jolly Good Fellow" to the birthday boy, who blows out twenty-seven candles. He cuts his birthday cake with a flourish, using a borrowed Mexican war sword.

Later, oh, much later, he privately confides to me: "I don't begrudge the broken arm—not one bit! It was all part of a glorious day and an even better evening." He gives my two hands a surreptitious squeeze—no one is watching. "You, of all people, know that I'm always ready to pay the piper when I've had a good dance … like I had today. *And* tonight. Every now and then, I like to drink the wine of life with brandy in it." So do I.

Sunday

15 November 1885

I could not even tell you.

Not even *you*, dear Woman's Journal. How full I am, how *ripe* with love, now that Theo is back in my life.

It's like he's never been gone, like the tragedy of Alice never happened.

(But it *did* happen, *I know it did,* and the memories will always be with him.)

Even so, he's reaching out for me now … so don't over-think things and take the hand he offers.

I've reached for pen and ink a million times. I think and think, but *still* … I just can't write about him. I can't put him on paper anymore. He's too alive for that. This afternoon, though, I'm *making* myself write because something momentous happened today, and I have to record it for posterity.

Usually somebody else is around when Theo and I are together: Mamma in the stuffed rocker by the front window, making mile after mile of ecru-colored tatting; Em at the dining room table, teaching herself Italian (gabbling verbs constantly and incorrectly–we're both in the process of learning, but I have a head start on her because of the lessons in Latin); or Mame constantly trotting to and fro, from kitchen to sideboard, sideboard to the coal-fired stove, answering the postman's ring at the door, putting together our next meal.

It's even worse at Bamie's Madison Avenue house, Theo's base of operations in the city. Even Fanny Smith Dana calls on him there (far too frequently for my liking). Her husband, Commander Dana, is seriously ill, and I can't help but think Fanny is already planning ahead for her next spouse.

Well, she can't have him. He has *my* heart now—even more than before—and I'd die before letting her nab him, because…

…today, for several hours, everyone was out of the house, and I had Theo all to myself. Also because…

…he kisses me today as we sit together in Mamma's S-shaped parlor loveseat, alone in the twilight, our hands entwined with each other's.

I kiss him back in exultation, meeting him more than halfway.

It feels like coming home. It *is* coming home. He kisses *me* back, again and again, over and over. Our arms slide up—well, two of my arms and only one of his because his broken arm is still in a sling—to embrace as the kisses deepen and become … well, audible.

Even Schatzi wakes up and starts whining.

We both laugh at the dog, even though it shatters the moment.

Then, the front door rattles, and Theo springs out of the chair like he's been shot. Just in time, too, for Em clomps in—with muddy boots, wouldn't you just know—and a greengrocer's parcel in her arms.

But in the chatter and clatter that follows, I can't help thinking: can he actually be thinking what I *think* he's thinking?

I can't always tell with Theo...

Does he just "want me for now?" Or ... does he value *and* want me "for keeps?" If it's the latter, then what about Italy?

MONDAY

16 NOVEMBER 1885

I taly ... oh, you magical place! ... upon which I've pinned *so* many of our family's hopes and dreams...

My hopes and dreams, especially.

Why did Theo decide to come back into my life *now?*

Is it worth it? Is *he* worth it—to me?

I'm spending today alone—no good deeds already planned, thank goodness. I remain secluded and sequestered in the house, mostly in my bedroom. I tell the family I'm feeling a bit "off" today and need to rest.

I keep thinking and thinking … as I take ever-shallower breaths and hunch my shoulders ever closer to my ears. I even scribble, putting pencil to paper, my lists of pros and cons: a life with Theo versus a life in Italy.

When I read the pages over, I groan, unsatisfied with any of it. I crumple the pages in frustration and indecision, flinging them into the cheerful, hard coal fire in the fireplace.

I start all over again with the pros … and then the cons…

I implore my inner self: *Let's pull no punches, take no prisoners … what* are *the cons if I hitched my star to Theo's? Be honest with me, self, because you know all would not be totally "rosy" in a life with Theo. Much as I love him, he has "detriments" aplenty—even as I have.*

I chew on a sharp, no. 2 pencil thoughtfully and then list them.

CONS:

1. *I'm not Alice—undeniable fact.*

2. *I'll never be as beautiful, popular, or all-around "sunny" as she was. Will this undeniable fact be more than he could eventually bear?*

3. *I don't like politics. I don't like political gossip or deep political arguments. What kind of a way is that for a wife to be, especially when one's husband is on a trajectory for the political universe?*

4. *Theo is an absolute innocent, a rube, about money. Always being rich, he never knows what it's like to have to scrimp and save, beg and barter, or rob Peter to pay Paul. He could (and would) easily run through the family's money in no time. I'd always have to keep firm hold of the family purse strings, allowing none to trickle through my fingers without my own express decision and doing.*

5. *Theo loves to dress in bright colors and silly styles. He requires a wife who will check*

and "approve" (or correct) his style of dress
before he goes off to work.

6. Theo's sisters will always be subconsciously
jealous of any woman who draws his
attention away from the two of them. I'd
just have to live with that.

7. Theo needs to be constantly "moving" or
"doing"—there would be little peace in
such a marriage and little time in which to
settle down or even draw the next breath.
What would such a tumultuous marriage
do to the possibility of … the new possible
me? She doesn't exist just yet, and maybe
won't exist at all. It all depends. She is still
yet to be formed … a version of myself that
exists in the ether of possibilities: Edith
Kermit Carow, noted oil painter and
premiere sketch artist, writer of intelligent
contemporary poetry and substantive essays,
a happily independent single woman living
in an expat community along the beautiful
Italian Riviera.

If I married Theo, this version of Edie would never exist ... never come into being ... never have a chance to try her wings...

TUESDAY

17 NOVEMBER 1885

For good or ill ... this day will live in my heart forever.

In the misty November chill of Riverside Park, Theodore Roosevelt II, with his arm still in a sling ... again, after so *very* many years and so many miles, we each have traveled alone ... asked me to marry him.

Suddenly, I could not breathe.

A faint, misty vision of Edie, the Italian-based artist, shimmered before my vision. The tantalizing, sunny vision glimmered irresistibly. Simultaneously, I realize it's naught but possibility—one of a million possibilities that may or may not ever materialize.

Standing before me, Theo is actuality. I hear a voice … *my* voice … saying, "I love you."

"Um, does that mean yes?" Theo smiles a bit nervously. He needs clarification.

"Yes! Yes, it does!" My voice speaks of its own accord. My inner self has nothing to do with it. Destiny spoke for me, and suddenly, I mean it with all my heart.

I feel about to embark on a grand and momentous journey.

As I truly am—I know it deep in my bones.

Goodbye dear Edie of Italy and to all your hopes, dreams, and possibilities. They'll remain in the ether now, unexpressed in this lifetime. Hello to the new Edie … Edie Roosevelt … mother of children, wife of the newest rising star in the political firmament, and lover and partner of the only man she ever wanted.

After a lengthy kiss and burst of excited laughter, I remind him that I *will still* be moving my family to Italy and getting them settled in before we head off on our honeymoon. The only difference will be … that I will not be moving in *with* them, as earlier planned.

We decide to keep our engagement a secret from *everyone* for a while. That means *all* family, friends, servants, neighbors, and most assuredly the insatiable political press.

I'm all too aware that Theo *must* abide (insofar as possible) with society's mandate of a long period of mourning for Alice Lee. Society and politics would both scorn and shun him if he didn't. Now he is fully aware that I *too* must fulfill responsibilities for my widowed mother, aging servant, and awkward sister before I can move forward into my own new married life.

I also remind him to keep Italy a secret, too. "I beg you *not* tell Bamie, Conie, or even Aunt Annie about this, nor about the sale of our house—*nobody*, not just yet. *No* one needs to know for the present. Mamma and I agree on one thing, and that is we both dread to look like *fools* if our grandiose plans should come to naught."

I tell him the rest of the Italy plan ... how the house sale money will even provide for a side trip to England so Mamma can look up distant cousins before we continue on to Italy. "We've already wired a deposit to the Bonner Hotel, a modest—and supposedly respectable—rooming house in London. Mamma wants to stay there at least six months, so I've promised her that all of us shall—I mean ... why not?"

Theo agrees. "Then I'll meet and marry you in London, as soon as we can."

"It will have to be a year from now," I remind him, even as my heart sinks and the bottom drops out of my stomach.

He tries to reassure me. "At least the period of mourning won't have to be five years, only three years these days. The times, they are changing. Everything goes faster nowadays!"

That reminds me of something serious and sober, possibly irrevocable.

I can't stop myself from bringing it up.

"You..." I stammer a bit but make myself continue.

"You once told Elliott and the girls—and the girls told *me*—that you don't approve of second marriages. You said they're the sign of … a weak and unworthy character."

There, I've said it.

Have I smashed everything to bits again? The way I did before?

He has the decency to look abashed, but still he answers me in a low voice.

"And I was right. I *don't* approve of second marriages. But with you … I just can't help myself, Edie. I *know* I'm weak, spineless, and shameful, but I can't help reviving that spark of love that once existed between us, so long ago now. I loved you then … and I'm loving you now."

(He looks surprised by his own words, but, bless his heart, he forges on.)

"I'm blowing on those embers of love right now, Edie. Can you feel the warmth? The fire of our first love? And our new love to come?"

All I can do is nod. My eyes fill with tears, and my lips assume a tremulous grin. Then we're kissing and embracing, again and again, over and over. I'm crying and laughing at the same time, and so, even, is Theo.

I decide, then and there, to start calling my darling Theo by his true given name, Theodore, because we are both "being made anew," as the Bible says.

Theodore—it suits him.

He pulls from his pocket a sapphire engagement ring, a little gold watch, and his mother's pearl necklace.

For the meantime, I'll wear the engagement ring around my neck on my long, thin gold chain—I already have something that will suffice—and hide all "evidence" under my corset cover.

17 November is a day that will live in my heart, always—a day that marks the end of Edie Carow's life and the birth of a new entity, Edie Roosevelt … Mrs. Edith Kermit Carow Roosevelt. It's the end of Edie the artist in Italy. She never had a chance to exist…

Sometimes … in the middle of the night (*often*, truth be told), I know I'm *still* going to think about Alice Lee and Edie the artist in Italy.

Alice—so tall, blonde, and beautiful. She's no longer in an earthly existence but always remembered and revered. Edie the artist in Italy was never yet for real but always a possibility … could I have "made something of myself" as an artist? I will never know now.

Can Theodore truly … ever? … get over Alice? Has he just turned pragmatic? Eager to start that "big family" he always said he wants— and am I just a known quantity who just happens to be … a handy vessel?

◆◆ ◆ ◆◆

TUESDAY

1 DECEMBER 1885

The morning *Times* reports that the U.S. Patent Office acknowledges this date in history as when the favorite southern beverage "Dr. Pepper" is "served in public at various venues" for the very first time, including New York City.

We just *have* to try it, Theodore and I!

We head over to Arnold Constable's Marble Palace at 280 Broadway, north of City Hall Park between Chambers and Reade Streets. It's *such* an elegant store with so many different departments, five stories tall. I'd never been in there before—*far* too expensive for the likes of me.

As a promotional stunt, Marble Palace is offering free samples of Dr. Pepper to the shopping public. Store employees fill countless shot glasses with the enticing, bubbling, brown liquid while crowds of shoppers come forward to "sample the wares." (Young boys in the background keep washing and drying used shot glasses, then returning them to where they are refilled again as the crowds surge forward.)

Over and over, employees are careful to reassure the public, "No, there is *no* alcohol in this drink whatsoever. It is perfectly safe for women and children, too."

Of course, the store has cases and cases of Dr. Pepper in actual glass bottles that one can purchase if they enjoy the free sample.

What do *I* think of Dr. Pepper? It's biting, yet sweet—*too* sweet for my taste. After Theodore tries his free sample, all he says is, "Interesting!" We don't buy any to take home, but it's great fun to sample it just the same.

Thursday

Near midnight on Christmas Eve 1885

He still hasn't changed his mind.

He *still* wants to marry me. He's promised *not* to escape into Dakota Territory again for a *long* time to come.

It's all so surreal, unnerving, even, as if so many years haven't passed (but they have) and harsh words were never spoken (but they were).

Still … I'm hanging on to this precious "nevertheless" in my life for all its worth.

Whatever happened before, I'm not looking back. I plan to make a life—a strenuous, exciting, and unpredictable life—with this man.

Come what may.

SUNDAY

14 FEBRUARY 1886

It's Valentine's Day. I haven't written in ages (there's been no *time!*), but today I just had to. I commemorate this day as the Roosevelt time of untimely death and pain. The death of dear Greatheart ... of Alice Lee Roosevelt ... the time of year when Theo once wrote "the light went out of my life" (and his heart).

Purposely, I involve myself in other plans for today—taking Mamma and Em to an Episcopal Church high tea—so I can give Theo plenty of space and privacy, in which to grieve and move on.

I can't even think of him grieving without experiencing visceral pain … right around the area of my heart.

I will write more tomorrow.

Theodore and I see each other nearly every day—thank goodness, and what a *whirl*—plays, dinners, horseback rides in Central Park, balls, the opera, and so much more.

We send daily written messages when we're apart. (Neither of us trusts the telephone, though we admit it can be convenient at times.)

It pleases me no end to have others tell me how "very bored and restless Theo seems to be when he's forced to socialize *without* his old chum Edie."

We often join up with friends—the more, the better. All the better to hide our secret connection behind a smokescreen of jokes, teasing, nonchalance, and humor.

Even Mrs. Will Dana—the former Fanny Smith, who still gushes and flutters her eyelashes shamelessly at Theo despite the proximity of her own long-suffering husband—even *she* considers us as benignly "brother and sister." *(Good.)*

Elliott, Bamie, and Conie have taken to calling their elder brother by their late father's old "pet" name—Thee.

No one suspects us—and believe me, I'd *know*. I keep an eagle eye (and ear) out for any sign of "knowingness" in our friends and family.

I take that back—Em is starting to suspect, although I blithely scoff and laugh off her speculations. I have to say … Em seems to be growing into a perceptive confidant.

I'll have to tell them eventually, of course—Em, Mamma, and Mame, especially before we board the steamships, the first one bound for England and then, a few months later, a ferry across the Channel, and a train bound for the Italian Riviera. Only three of "us" will take that as their final journey's end—after settling the family in, I'll turn away on a separate journey with my new bridegroom. What do we do in the daytime, Theo and I? We work! *Hard.* Especially Theodore, keeping abreast of the political scene, both state and national. Plus, he writes heaps of articles—for money. Poor dear! The blasted cattle sucked up most of his inheritance, and now he has to work for a living like the rest of us.

Theodore may be a genius with a photographic memory, but he's the town dunce with money. Ten dollars in his pocket at breakfast literally vanishes by dinnertime—usually given away to good causes or people in need or spent on new silk pocket hankies (fashion slave that he is).

By day, I keep up with my charitable work … teaching needlework to immigrant girls … helping youngsters learn to read English … still helping serve dinner occasionally at the Newsboys' Lodging House, even as Greatheart did so many years ago now.

I also spend *hours*—daily—preparing for the great Carow migration. I work closely with Mr. Cruikshank, Papa's accountant, to set up Mamma's annuity and our house-sale nest egg to be readily available, first in London and then later in Italy by January 1887. Today, with mixed feelings and butterflies in my stomach, I purchased four second-class steamship tickets on the Inman Line for a mid-sized, iron-hulled, screw-propelled ship built in 1881 and christened (appropriately) as *City of Rome*. It leaves New York Harbor on 15 March, just thirty days from today.

LATER:

I also made arrangements with Mr. Cruikshank for him to wire a deposit for three bedrooms (one for Em and me, another for Mamma, and an "upgraded" servant's room for Mame) at the modestly priced but still "eminently respectable" Bucklands Hotel in London—a genteel rooming house masquerading as a hotel.

Still, we tell *no one*—it's silly, I know, but I figure it's nobody's business but our own until we feel like spilling the beans ourselves. Mamma has very few friends to inquire about such things, anyway, and I readily change the subject away from "private matters" when out in public.

Even Bamie and Conie have only the vaguest idea … something about "the Carows visiting relatives in England this summer, perhaps?" They know nothing about the house sale … the *blessed* house sale … that's paying for the steamship tickets, paying for the London "holiday with family," and generating future interest against remaining principal to pay the pensione rent in Italy each month while Mamma's annuity covers day-to-day costs.

Mame will have to help with day-to-day finances in Italy because *I* won't be there. I'll be with—

(Again, I feel butterflies in my stomach, but they are happy butterflies this time.)

SATURDAY

13 MARCH 1886

Theo and I spent part of *everyday* together. It's been Heaven for me … and I hope for him, too. But I can't think about that just now, because—

(I'm gagging with "nerves" … more about this in a minute…)

May the Lord bless Henry Cabot Lodge twelve ways until Sunday! He pulled some strings so that Theo can start writing the biography of Senator Thomas Hart Benton for Houghton Mifflin Company. The publishing house will bestow Theo with a lavish sum once it's done—plus, there should be royalties, too. But I can't think about this now because—

(My stomach now feels like a hemp rope, knotted and pulled tighter, still tighter. I feel sick enough to upchuck.)

Theo's managers at his new Elkhorn Ranch—the erstwhile Maine guides, Sewall and Dow—are, according to Theo, "awfully nervous and dispirited. I'm worried about them."

Apparently, the guides *still* think that western Dakota Territory is "*not* good country to sustain cattle," even though Theo assures me that "winter losses were minimal this year." He's very afraid the Maine men are going to "ask out" of their contracts, and he can ill afford to lose either man this summer. "You understand, don't you dearest? Why I must leave on the first Monday train for the west?"

I *do* understand. It's right and very sensible. Besides, it can't be helped. But—it'll be *nine entire months* before I see him again. *That's* what makes me so nervous and miserable.

Plus, there will be the entire Atlantic Ocean between us.

I think of Jack, which reminds me that *anything* can happen in nine months. A woman could have a baby, a man could marry a stranger, a person could end up in *jail* over the course of *nine months—anything* can happen.

Oh, I'll be pining and grieving all right, but it's all part of the agreement I made with myself. It's part of what I promised to do to become the new entity called Edie Roosevelt, my new identity. On behalf of the lost artist Edie of Italy, I'm going to give it *all I've got.*

LATER:

I finally vomited into the wash basin and feel all the better for it. I must clean it up tonight, though, so Mame won't think I intentionally left it for her in the morning.

I will write more about tomorrow … our last day, for now.

Sunday night

14 March 1886

I can't help it.

I asked Theo something dangerous today, on our very last day together for the next nine months. I *have* to know before we marry.

We visit all of our favorite spots in Riverside Park. (It's surprisingly warm—spring is early this year—with no wind at all.)

Sunset begins. A glorious sky radiates purple-and-gold glory over the white-winged sailboats on the Hudson River.

I check my little pendant watch—6:30 p.m. I know that Theo prearranged a hansom cab to meet us at 7 p.m. on the corner of West 79th Street and Riverside Drive to take us to our respective homes before it gets too dark.

Side by side, we stand, watching the sunset. His right arm holds me close along his body.

It's now or never—I *must* ask him, even though I dread to bring up such an indelicate subject at the last minute.

"Theodore…"

If I don't ask him now, I'll lose my nerve.

"Mmm?"

"Theodore, I'd like you to … step in front of me so I can … hug you from behind."

With a laugh he asked: "Tired of gazing at my visage already?"

"*Never!* But there's something I need to tell you, but it's … very hard to say. I want to tell you when you're not looking at me."

He obliges—with a Mona Lisa smile of his own, but one tinged with concern.

First, I bury my face against the back of his wool suit coat, wrapping my arms around his waist, which is more ample than it used to be—my bare fingers can barely clasp together.

I pivot my head to the right—so I can see something other than the wool of his coat. I stare into the growing twilight of Riverside Park's woods, and I begin.

"Theodore…" (I call him by his grown-up name now and vow to always do so in the future. If there *is* to be a future between us.)

"Theodore, *why* do you want to marry me?"

"*Why?*" he blurts, laughing and astonished. He tries to turn around to look at me, but I hang on tight and won't let him do it. "Because … well, because we just seem to belong together, don't you think? I *know* we can make a glorious life together—family, children, home, affection, honor—*all* of it." I think: *affection*. What a milquetoast word.

What about love? What about passion? What about Alice?

"Theodore…" I begin again. (I *have* to say it. I hope it won't wreck things again … won't shatter my future … to speak the truth, as I did before.)

"Theodore … darling … What I'm *trying* to say is, you've already had a…"—I swallow hard at this point but soldier on—"…a good marriage with an honorable, young lady and also, well, a physical relationship with her."

Theo stands stock-still. I feel him tense under my hands. After a long pause, he finally speaks: "Yes. But you *know*…"

His voice sounds thin and strained. "You *know* I've vowed never to speak about that time in my life, ever again."

"Nor should you, Theodore. That is private, for you alone. That is 'what went before'…"

Then "it all" riles up within me, and I can't stop myself.

"Dearest darling, there is one thing I *cannot* do in marriage, no matter what came before or what may come after…"

In a low voice, Theo asks, "And that is?"

"I cannot live with a ghost in my bed, in *our* bed, together."

There. I've said it.

Theo's sharp intake of breath is immediate.

I've wrecked it, yet again. I've wrecked it forever this time.

But I meant it. I'd say it again because it's true. There can *only* be two in our bed: him and me.

Yes, I know he had this other life. I know I can never compare to, compete with, or measure up to the ghost of the matchless Alice, even though I just *know* that if she'd lived, she'd start to bore him silly as time went on.

"Theodore, I love you *so* much. It would break my heart to know there would always be three in our bed. Dearest, I just couldn't bear it…" Now I'm crying, and it's not pretty. I snuffle and gulp, nearly gagging on the words.

"I would rather not marry you at *all* … rather than always be second best."

Theodore tries to turn around, but still I won't let him.

"I love you more than anyone else in the *world*, Theodore. You know that. *You* are my first, my last, and my best. But here's the thing. I know that you cannot truthfully say the same about *me*. It's a fact of life, and I know this. I know I'm asking a *huge* thing of you as you—as *we*—embark upon a new life. I ask that you not invite your…"

I swallow hard again, but my spoken words that follow are softer than before.

"…your beloved's spirit … to follow us into our future life together—and into our future bed. Because that's the only way I can ever marry you, Theodore. It's a life-altering decision, I know. You'll have a really long time—nine months—to decide what you want to do—how you want to live out the rest of your life."

Again, he tries to turn to face me, but now I'm too mortified. "Don't look at me, Theodore.

I'm *so* ashamed, but … I *had* to say it. You understand, don't you? … don't you, dearest?"

He remains quiet a long time. Then, he speaks so low I stop breathing for a moment so I can hear him. "Yes, I understand."

I press my cheek against the wool of his jacket. It's definitely tear-soaked now.

The sudden approach of the hansom cab causes us to move apart. Theo has a troubled, guilty expression on his face. I can only guess how swollen-faced and disheveled I must look.

"Here, Edie, you take the cab home, it's no trouble at all for me to walk."

I try to protest, but I'm too spent with emotion to be anything but ineffectual.

I fear that I've wrecked everything, again.

Then, I experience a wave of agony, knowing I won't see him again for nine more months— at the very least, *if* he doesn't change his mind. Maybe I'll never see him at *all*. Who knows?

"Be safe, my darling, be safe until we meet again in London." My chin quivers as I manage a watery smile and a last "I love you, Theodore."

He doesn't kiss me, at least not my lips. He bends over my clasped hands for the longest time, his lips pressed against my gloveless skin. "Goodbye, Edie dearest … until we meet again." Then he's gone, striding quickly into the dark city twilight.

He didn't say that he loved me, too.

He didn't say "until we meet again *in London*."

"Until we meet again"—that could mean anything, couldn't it?

It could mean London *or*—equally possibly—it could refer to a time, thirty or forty years hence, when we're both dead and meeting up beyond the veil.

I have nine months to find out if he's really going to show up and marry me.

Or not…

MONDAY MORNING

15 MARCH 1886

6:45 A.M.

I know he's boarding the train for the west right now.

I feel hollow and cautious—so much is unsure.

Yet, I also feel a tremulous happiness—tremulous yet persistent, resolute above all else. Whatever happens, I *will* marry him—even if I have to move forward on faith alone.

He says he loves me. He *seems* to love me. I love him.

Whatever the depth of his feeling for me—be it shallow, merely expedient ("she's handy"), something deeper, or as yet undetermined—I *will* marry him, come what may.

Despite the ever-present shadow of Alice. Despite the always-fawning Fanny Smith, who waits in the wings of his life. Despite the specter of Edie the artist in Italy, waiting to materialize into a life of her own.

Letters ... I must write to him *now*, immediately. I will not whine or beg reassurance from him of his "love." I begin the rest of my life now as I mean to go on. I mean to go on as his wife. Come what may.

TUESDAY

16 MARCH 1886

This woman's journal ... I just can't do it.

I can no longer write in this diary at present, especially anything about Theodore, our plans, and the physical distance between us.

It makes me too nervous and makes me start to *doubt*. I *cannot* start to doubt.

I must move forward and not think too much.

Until later, dear Journal, when I feel more confident. Until much, much later, because I don't want to "jinx" anything.

Instead, I'll start tackling our furniture today ... what (small) pieces to send directly on to Italy, what to sell, and what to put into temporary storage for my own (albeit tenuous) future married life, about which my family still guesses nothing.

SATURDAY

24 APRIL 1886

I can't sleep. It's not quite 5 a.m. The *City of Rome* leaves *today*, bound for Liverpool, England.

England. (Oh gosh … the butterflies are back in my stomach.)

We're in for it now—it's really happening. A new life awaits us across the sea.

Soon, there'll be more than six thousand miles between us. *Anything* can happen (and most generally does) when six thousand miles—and nine months—separate you from the one you love.

Conie thinks we're only "going away for eighteen months." I don't want to correct or clarify anything. It's best to keep things nebulous for a while. After all, Conie might turn out to be right.

I'm burying my woman's journal deep at the bottom of my valise and won't take it out until we arrive at the rooming house in London. Our time in Liverpool will be far too chaotic, what with outings and tours with cousins and the like. Be safe, dear Journal, until I see you again…

TUESDAY

8 JUNE 1886

London—we're finally *here*. I still can hardly believe it.

The ocean crossing was mostly cold and more than a little sea-sickish. I read a lot, and of course, there wasn't much to look at on the ocean … except ocean.

Liverpool is a grimy but bustling place, full of Mamma's second cousins and more, even further "removed." They make us feel very welcome, though, which causes Mamma to actually break into tears. We happily stay in Liverpool for the entire month of May in a dingy but clean hotel. I don't remember when I've seen Mamma so "chirked up," happy, and animated. Now, after a half-day train trip from Liverpool, we find ourselves in London! The June weather is simply gorgeous—I certainly wasn't expecting *this!*

Schatzi can again walk on terra firma, instead of quivering in a dog crate in the hold of the ship or on a train. Aboard ship, she only saw daylight—on a walking lead—four times a day to tend to her "business."

Home is now here at Bucklands Hotel at 43 Brook Street. Although a bit rundown at the heels, still it's a proper, modest place on the edge of fashionable Mayfair.

I write long, frequent letters to T, numbering each and every one to make sure he receives them all. (I think of Jack Traynor Stratton and the letter I sent him that he said "never arrived" … *did* it actually arrive, I wonder, and he was just trying to let me down easy?) I want to be sure Theodore reads my letters in proper sequence.

He writes to me, too—a *lot*, thank goodness. (Of course, he's an inveterate letter writer—he can't help himself.)

He mentions the weather a lot, *and* cows. Cattle are much on his mind. He doesn't send many romantic musings.

I write volumes back to him. His letter of 24 May scolded me that he'd only heard from me once after he'd sent me seventeen letters— although I've only received fourteen of these to date. I've sent him *twenty-one letters* thus far. Hopefully he'll soon receive a huge packet of my letters all at once. Mail service in the wilds of Dakota Territory must not be very efficient.

I can't help writing this to him—he always brings out the bare-faced truth in me:

You know that I love you so much and would do anything in the world to please you. I wish I could be sure my letters sound as much like myself as yours do, exactly

*like you. You know all about me, darling.
I never could love anyone else. I love you
with all the passion of a girl who has never
loved before, so please be patient with me
when I don't know how to "put my heart
on paper." Please love me and know that
I think of you all the time and want so
much to see you. Mamma and Emily ask
me to send you their love, and you know
you have all of your*

… Edith

I wish…

I wonder what he's doing right this moment.
I hope he's hard at work on that biography of
Thomas Hart Benton for Houghton Mifflin
Company—he certainly needs the money.

I received a much-battered but *delectable*
packet of letters from the United States

today, from my darling, of course, and some from Conie and Bamie, too.

Yes, dearest T finally finished the last pages of *Benton* at his Elkhorn Ranch. I can just see him, getting up every day at dawn … sitting at his desk … writing as fast as he can while the morning air is still cool and bearable. By noon, the ranch house must be too baking-hot to endure, but endure he must.

He writes that heat waves shimmer over everything. The grass is prematurely brown. Mrs. Sewall's vegetable garden is wilting, and they can't keep up with the hand-watering. A feeling of foreboding lies over the West like a burial shroud.

On 2 July, Conie had her second baby: a girl. She names her Corinne Douglas Robinson, but they're already calling her Corinney.

On the Fourth of July in Dakota Territory, T writes that "the temperature is nearly 120 degrees today, and an oven-like wind blows through the Dakotas, killing every green thing, except for the leaves on a few riverside trees."

He takes the train to Dickinson to celebrate the one hundred and tenth anniversary of the Declaration of Independence with the townspeople, who choose him as Orator of the Day. His letter says that he "can see people converging from all points of the compass, on foot, on horseback, and in old-style covered wagons." It's the largest crowd ever assembled in Dakota Territory, "and most of them are already drunk." At 10 a.m., the parade gets underway. The Declaration of Independence is read aloud in the public square, followed by everyone singing "My Country 'Tis of Thee." The crowd adjourns to the town hall for a "free lunch" (probably crackers). Soon after, the master of ceremonies, Dr. Stickney, introduces the afternoon's speakers. "The Honorable Theodore Roosevelt" stands up last, to rousing cheers of acclaim and affection.

He gives his speech, the highlights of which he quotes to me in his letter: "Like all Americans, I like big things ... big prairies, big forests and mountains ... big wheat fields and railroads, and herds of cattle, too ... big factories, steamboats, and everything else. But we must keep steadily in mind that no people were ever yet benefited by riches of their prosperity that also corrupted their virtue. Each one of us *must* do his part if we wish to show that this nation is worthy of its good fortune." After his speech, everyone heads over to the dirt racetrack to watch "the Cowboys take on the Indians" at the horse races.

One other item of note. On the train ride back to Medora that evening, T and a local newspaper editor sit and talk as the train rumbles along, watching the fireworks explode into the darkening sky behind them … "and I confess my longing to him to return to public life. I believe I can do my best work in a public and political way. Then the editor says to me in a serious voice, 'Believing as you do, then I believe you'll eventually become President of the United States.' I consider the many ramifications of this statement and answer the editor, 'If your prophecy comes true, I will do my best to be a good one.'"

Thursday

29 July 1886

I finally decide to tell Mamma, Emily, and Mame about … the secret engagement.

It turns out, they'd guessed all along, but they didn't want to say anything until *I* did.

Mamma admits she is very nervous about moving to Italy with just Emily and Mame by her side. I reassure them, over and over, that I'll "come along with you and get you *fully* settled in before doing anything else—I *promise.*"

I send Theodore a letter confirming our wedding on 2 December 1886 at St. George's Anglican Church in London.

It still seems so ephemeral and unreal. It has to be real. It *will* be real.

It *has* to be, else … what will I do?

SUNDAY

22 AUGUST 1886

Letters continue to fly from one shore of the Atlantic to the other. Summer is crowded with events on both sides of the ocean—some momentous and others happily trivial.

Bamie buys a new house, gains weight, and then travels to Mexico—there is no evident correlation between these facts whatsoever!

Baby Lee stays with her grandparents at Chestnut Hill. (Good for many reasons. The Lees must miss their sunny daughter so keenly; I cannot comprehend such pain.)

Still ever the social playboy, Elliott keeps busy on the society scene with his wife, the beautiful Anna, and their homely little daughter, Eleanor. Nell plans to build his family a new house on Long Island. We'll see...

T left the West unexpectedly for a quick working trip to NYC. A job he looked into with the New York Board of Health didn't work out because the incumbent refused to resign, even after being officially indicted for corruption.

T then spent three weeks at the Astor Library, checking facts in his Thomas Hart Benton manuscript before relinquishing it to Houghton Mifflin. Then, he got back on the next train to the Badlands, his mind still uneasy. He writes that the "future looks dim ahead for me" as far as politics goes. "I know my destiny must lie somewhere—but *where?*"

(Dear God, I hope I'm not a millstone around his neck. I hope I'm not a promise he regrets he ever made. I hope … so many things.)

At the Elkhorn Ranch, Mrs. Sewall gives birth to a baby boy, and Mrs. Dow is delivered of a son of her own, just one week later. What a happy tumult must reign there at the Elkhorn Ranch house with two new babies, plus little Kitty Sewall—the mountains of laundry, crying newborns, the bustle and din of family life. All this must remind T every minute of his current single state and engender in him a sense of … what? Restlessness, maybe? (That maybe he wishes he hadn't promised himself to a spinster more than six thousand miles away?)

Uncle Jimmie. No other person is to be told a word about it. I will explain everything in full when I see you, forever your loving brother. I shall return 6 October."

Although we've all been friends together for a quarter-century—quite literally—Bamie and Conie probably are *not* overjoyed at the prospect of me marrying their big brother, who they idolize. They always tell me (with fond bluntness) that I have a "possessive nature," and they probably fear I'll monopolize T all to myself—as I will, if I can—and claim a closer place to his heart than that of his cherished sisters.

A kettle of fish, this is, to be dealt with at some future time.

Friday

8 October 1886

The other shoe finally dropped.

Theodore's Maine guide ranch managers, Mr. Sewall and Mr. Dow, asked to "pack it in" (terminate their contracts), "cash themselves out" (get their money and go), and return home to Maine (which they're only too glad to do).

Theo confides to me in his last letter that "Sewell and Dow, alas, aren't able to sell the fall shipment of 'beeves' profitably. The best price Chicago will offer is *ten dollars less* than the cost of raising the animal in the first place. Plus, the cost of transporting each animal is even more."

Sewell and Dow both earnestly explain to Theodore that, by persisting in the cattle business, they're throwing away his money and that "the quicker the boss gets out of here, the less he will lose."

Theodore now agrees with this conclusion.

His $85,000 Badlands cattle investment— *eighty-five thousand dollars* ... such an *unfathomable* amount of money in *my* modest world!—erodes away by the minute. He asked the original ranch managers, Bill Merrifield and Sylvane Ferris, still at the Maltese Cross, if they'll also take over the Elkhorn herd. In future, he'll use the new ranch house only as a "stopover place" to check on cattle or as a hunting base.

He already asked Sewall and Dow, "How soon can you go?" They're now in the process of squaring accounts with one another.

Meanwhile, a soft, blue-gray haze settles over the Badlands, reducing trees and cattle to pale ghosts. The strangeness makes the cowboys and animals very uneasy. Official weather forecasters dismiss the haze as "accumulation of fumes from the grass fires that smolder all summer on the tinder-dry plains."

But the cowboys and animals know better.

Although it's still baking-hot, old-timers are starting to lay in a six-month supply of winter provisions. Everyone says: "Nature is fixing up her folks for hard times ahead." Beavers work constantly to thicken their lodges. Muskrats grow extra-thick coats and build their houses twice the usual height.

Theodore writes, "I myself noticed the wild geese and songbirds hurrying south many weeks earlier than usual."

Sewall and Dow, along with their wives, babies, and baggage, plan to lock up the place and leave—for good—on 15 October. Theodore will leave for Manhattan a week before that, because … politics is calling him, once again.

He says he'll write and tell me all about it as soon as he knows more—"It's a promise I made to Republican headquarters, and I must honor it"—before he finally boards the steamship, crosses the Atlantic, and enfolds me in his arms in London.

Oh T, *please* don't get yourself involved in some political scheme just before our wedding!

Friday

15 October 1886

Homesickness for NYC stabs at me this fine London morning. Much-delayed copies of Manhattan papers (arriving in London about five days late) trumpet some surprising news. For the first time in NYC history, a newly formed *Labor Party* will confront—and bitterly fight—both Republicans and Democrats alike.

What's more, the Labor Party candidate is the dangerous Henry George, said to be the "most powerful radical in America."

What's even *worse*, my own T agreed to serve as the "sacrificial lamb" of the Republican Party. Not only will he go up against Henry George, but he'll also face the powerful Abram S. Hewitt, the Democratic candidate, to lead our great city. Hewitt is ... well, he's absolutely *perfect:* a successful captain of industry in vigorous middle age, bolstered by vast wealth, popular opinions, impeccable refinement, and flawless breeding.

T writes to me that Hewitt "is also famous for his enlightened attitude toward labor" ... which causes my dearest to grouse and moan on the page, "And that's supposed to be *my* political niche!"

But T has no choice in the matter. Earlier on, he promised the party, "If you need me for anything—and I do mean *anything*—you've only to ask, and I'll hasten forward quickly there!" The Republican Party is taking him at his word.

They've taken him aside, so to speak, and advised him (in so many words): "Mr. Roosevelt, you've promised us, and frankly, you owe us one. We need a respectable, virtuous candidate who is willing to *lose* this time around. And that's going to be *you*. We're asking you to shore up the Party so it retains credibility and respect. Then, when you're older, you can come back and *win*."

Theodore agrees. After all, he gave his word. I think … *what if he* wins?

There goes our blissful three-month honeymoon!

(Yes, dear Journal, I'm *well* aware that Alice Lee had a *five*-month honeymoon with Theodore. But that was "before cattle"—he had a lot more money then. We both must watch his pocketbook carefully now.)

If he wins, he and I must return to New York City before 1 January.

He's so persuasive, he *might* win after all. He's strong, good, wise, and irresistible … how could anyone not vote for him?

Oh T, *please* don't win … at least not this time.

WEDNESDAY

27 OCTOBER 1886

It's T's twenty-eighth birthday, and *I* aim to celebrate it—where else?—at the theater. (I should write "theatre," as they do here in England.)

Mamma, Em, Mame, and I managed to snag ourselves tickets to *The Mikado* at the grand Savoy Theatre, built not long ago as a special showcase to Gilbert and Sullivan productions.

We were lucky to get tickets at *all*, it's such a fiercely popular show. What's especially cunning and exciting is that the theatre is *entirely lit up by electric lights—all* of it, not just on stage—which everyone knows make things "cooler and cleaner." Sitting amid gaslights in summer can be hugely uncomfortable!

We here in London are five hours ahead of New York, so T still has several hours to go yet before he announces his candidacy for Mayor of New York City (as a sacrificial lamb). He's going to make the announcement from the steps of Cooper Union, the wonderful progressive school, college, and gathering area founded by that true angel of a man, Peter Cooper. Only an angel would make this school *free* for the working classes, even for *women*, too! There has never been a "color bar" at Cooper Union. Blacks, Chinese, and even members of Indian tribes are *all* welcome to speak in public here and also to learn without paying tuition. Even Abraham Lincoln himself, totally unknown in New York at the time, was invited to speak there and soon rose to great heights.

Theodore is the most progressive politician *I've* ever seen, and this treasured, progressive school will stand behind dear T all the more, once he gets going in his career.

I envision the dozens of bonfires tonight, bathing the historic Cooper Union building in a golden glow.

I can almost hear the crowds roaring as he enters the scene: "Three cheers for the next Mayor of New York!"

THURSDAY

28 OCTOBER 1886

Today's the day when France's fabulous new gift to America will finally be unveiled, after putting *all* the pieces together from the twenty hundred and fourteen different crates—the Statue of Liberty herself. Hundreds of sightseeing boats shall no doubt cover the bay. *How* I wish I were there to see it!

Only five more days until the mayoral election ... please, dear heart, *do not win!*

FRIDAY

29 OCTOBER 1886

In a letter dated 23 October—only six days ago! U.S. Mail is now fleeter than Mercury's wings—Bamie writes to me: "Dear Brother campaigns with all his strength, working eighteen hours a day and with three to five political meetings every night! It is such happiness to see him at his very *best* once more. Ever since he was out of politics in any active form, it has been a real heart sorrow to me. He always made more of his life than any man I ever knew. This is the first time since his Assembly days that he has enough work to keep him exerting all of his powers. Father possessed the same powers, only in a different way. I would never say or write any of this, except to you, but it is very restful to feel how you care for him and how happy he is in his devotion to you."

(Did Bamie just write "devotion?" How Theodore's *devotion* to me makes her feel "restful?" I feel a sudden horse-kick in my stomach, and … I feel so low and suddenly bleak. Where is the romance, drama, and glamour like he had with Alice? Apparently, I don't exude sufficient "romance" to be sufficiently noticed by anybody—let alone my popular suitor. Will Bamie and Conie … and Theodore … always pine for Alice—the golden ray of sunshine that once graced all of their lives?)

LATER:

Second best or not, I'm *still* going to marry him … if he'll still have me.

Even if I am merely a sensible (yet curvy) spinster—hardly anyone's ray of sunshine—yet I *am* still worthy of love. I know I am—even *his* love. I'll spend the rest of my life proving this to him, if he'll let me.

TUESDAY

2 NOVEMBER 1886

It's election day for mayor of the greatest city on Earth!

I'm in an agony of suspense: how's it going so far?! Thank Heaven, news this important *does* rate transmission along the transatlantic cable!

MUCH LATER:

New Yorkers came out en masse to vote. One press report stated that "peace and good humor prevailed around the ballot boxes, and early returns point to Abram S. Hewitt as the winner."

Thank Heaven.

WEDNESDAY

3 NOVEMBER 1886

Not so fast.

Theodore *might* truly have won after all, but for some eleventh-hour corruption and underhanded dealings within his own party.

The truth is only now starting to seep out, even all the way over to London.

Apparently, around 2 p.m. New York time, someone (unidentified) started circulating written notes within Republican headquarters that "it's official—Henry George's vote is going to be higher than expected and Roosevelt's lower than expected."

Party bosses shot back their secret replies to everyone on down the line: "All Republicans who haven't voted yet must immediately switch allegiance and vote *only* for Hewitt because, above all else, Henry George *must* be stopped."

The press reports I read today also added, "Mr. Roosevelt eventually became aware of this action." Oh, T ... how devastated you must feel, betrayed and used as an "expediency" by your own party, who "sold you out" (even for understandable reasons).

One article also said, "Mr. Roosevelt remained good-humored, going out to dinner with friends, being as buoyant as ever, even when it became plain that his defeat became a rout when more than fifteen thousand Republicans defected over to Hewitt." The voting result was ultimately:

Hewitt – 90,552

George – 68,100

Roosevelt – 60,435

I'm just so glad it's *over.* I'm so glad he *lost.*

Thursday

4 November 1886

The New York mayor's race continues to reverberate on both sides of the Atlantic. The press now treats my dear one with respect, kindness, and even affection. (Even press people who usually detest him.)

One of them—I forget now who—even wrote: "Who knows what may happen some other year, Mr. Roosevelt? Congressman, Governor, Senator, even President?"

(As if!)

If there hadn't been a "panic swing" to Hewitt, Theodore *might* have actually ... won.

Another report reads: "Men may rise on stepping stones of their dead selves to higher things."

Still another from the *Daily Graphic* suggests: "Reflect on this Tennysonian thought, Mr. Roosevelt, and may your slumbers be disturbed only by dreams of a nomination for the governorship, or maybe the presidency, in the impending by and by." (This from a reporter who is usually snide and mean.)

Theodore is quoted as saying, "All that I hope for, at best, is to make a good run and get out the Republican vote." Although he lost the election, his well-run campaign is already increasing his exposure and solidifying his party credentials.

LATER:

There's a rap at the door, very late.

A telegram from T:

LOOKING FORWARD TO SMALL
PRIVATE WEDDING LONDON
ON 2 DECEMBER (STOP) BAMIE
TRAVELING WITH ME TO
LIVERPOOL TO VISIT FRIENDS
(STOP) CONIE SENDS LOVE
BUT CANNOT TRAVEL DUE TO
IMMINENT FAMILY ADDITION
(STOP) LEAVING ON SS ETRURIA
SAT 6 NOVEMBER ARRIVE

LIVERPOOL THEN TRAIN TO
LONDON 13 NOVEMBER (STOP)
GLAD I LOST ELECTION (STOP)

YOUR OWN LOVER THEODORE

A scrap of yellow paper to keep forevermore.

SUNDAY

7 NOVEMBER 1886

He's on his way. Nine months passed in a blue-white flash.

My future looms with alarming immediacy. Six more days until he arrives.

Then I'll really *know…*

SATURDAY

JUST BEFORE MIDNIGHT

13 NOVEMBER 1886

He wired that he's here. He's "ready"—as ready as I am.

Trying in vain to stay calm and busy, I can't help jumping up every two seconds at imagined taps at the front door.

Em sees him first, though, from an upper window. She sees him sprint from the corner, where a cab drops him off, down the street toward the Bucklands Hotel. (He sends the cab on ahead with his luggage to Brown's Hotel, where he reserved bachelor quarters.)

"He's here, he's *here!*" Em shrieks. Mamma, Mame, and Em suddenly fly into a dither. (And so do other guests at the rooming house. News travels fast in a small establishment like this one.)

Ahead of the other Carow females, I race down the stairs and fling open the front door before any housemaid can get near it. (My family proceeds more slowly, kindly granting me a bit of privacy and elbow room to greet Theo.) Suddenly, there he is—solid, beloved, loving, and somehow terrifying.

All I can say is, "Hello, stranger!" I can't help but fling my arms around him, while he does the same to me. I'm embarrassed to find myself dissolving into happy tears.

"Hey, what's this?" He smiles at me and then kisses me, again and again.

His grin broadens—all white teeth and beautiful, perfectly formed, mirror-imaged lips. "Let's *do* this thing, shall we, dearest?"

I turn off the waterworks and grin back at him in agreement. "Yes, *let's!*"

Whatever degree of love we each happen to inhabit at this moment, it's going to be all right.

I just *know* it.

WEDNESDAY

1 DECEMBER 1886

Theodore and I are now *supremely* happy together at Brown's, his quarters just a couple of blocks from Bucklands.

Unlike the clean but rickety Bucklands, Brown's Hotel is discreet and *so* luxurious, a perfect setting for our reunion, with heavy lace curtains and plush drapes that shut out the rest of the world and so many dim, cozy alcoves, perfect for embraces.

Here … and here alone … we cuddle together on the settee before a roaring fire. Only here, alone together, can we express the secrets of our heart … and all of the intimacies I'd been unable to truly express in my letters.

So private were we in those first days when he arrived … keeping to ourselves in the dim privacy of T's rooms … that we managed to infuriate the American Ambassador by neglecting to tell him of our "dual presence" here in London. After all, T is now a well-known politician and literary figure. He's expected to do a lot of "man-to-man socializing" with British politicians, famous writers, publishers, and even members of royalty.

So that tongues don't wag too much, I spend a lot of time with the Carow women while my darling socializes with the political set. I keep Mamma, Em, and Mame company—and keep them busy, sewing lace onto my understated-yet-elegant wedding dress.

Bamie finally concludes her visits with her Bulloch uncles and old friends in Liverpool. She takes the train down to London and joins the wedding party.

Theodore's new friend from the steamship, "Springy"—Cecil Spring-Rice—comes to call. Even I, not one to immediately take new acquaintances to my bosom, adore him immediately. He's such a kindred spirit! He's going to be T's best man at the wedding.

Springy makes sure I'm invited to join the men on frequent outings all over southern England. T says, "It makes me feel like I'm living in one of Thackeray's novels."

We meet many of the intellectuals of the day, and T can truthfully say he's had lunch or dinner with them all.

T also shows me part of a letter he's about to send to Conie, who should be having another baby any day now. He writes: "You have no idea how sweet Edith is about so many different things. I don't think even I knew how wonderfully good and unselfish she is because she is naturally reserved and finds it especially hard to express her feelings to me on paper."

It's finally happening.

Tomorrow is my wedding day—*our* wedding day.

I still find it amazing to think it even possible … after so many years and after so much sorrow between us.

I think of the incident of the two mating dogs, oh, *so* many years ago now! I see them in my mind's eye—their urgency and eagerness to join into single union—and I think: *I won't* really *know it's real until … then.*

11 A.M., JUST AFTER OUR WEDDING BREAKFAST AT BROWN'S HOTEL

THURSDAY

2 DECEMBER 1886

St. George's Church of Hanover Square, London

It's our wedding day—the first day … and first night … of our new future life.

I'm just grabbing a few minutes to write some "wedding mementos" after our (elegant!) wedding breakfast at Brown's Hotel.

I want to get it all down: my impressions, hopes, dreams, but most of all, the fact of T's orange gloves (!!!), a last-minute gift from Springy just before the ceremony.

Over and over, I remind the Carow women, "Now, remind me, *please* … and make sure that *I* pack—or *somebody* packs!—my journal, along with my hand luggage, before we board the train for Dover. It *has* to go with the hand luggage, not the gray trunk, nor the black one, because they're being shipped straight on to Italy."

"Don't *worry!*" Em keeps telling me. Her voice drones on soothingly, a bridesmaid automaton. "Don't you worry. Among the four of us, we'll get it right. You're not to worry about a *thing.*"

(But that's what I do best—worry. It's my job as caretaker of the Carow family. But I can't stop to worry about caretaking now. I must write down the brief, amusing tale that is our wedding.)

It all starts at dawn today, with wedding nerves, of course. I'm up with the birds (yes, that too). There's pea soup *fog* outside, like I've never seen before.

Can Bamie make it over here through this impenetrable fog?

No worries—apparently Londoners take fog in stride. All you need to do is order yourself some "link bearers," and that's just what Bamie did from her hotel to where we're staying over at Bucklands. Link bearers are official, hired men with knotted ropes who help paying strangers find their way in the fog from Point A to Point B. Who would have thought it?

Bamie, Mame, Mamma, and Em help me into my Valenciennes-lace gown and orange-blossom-studded veil. (I shoot a quick glance toward the mirror and see a stranger looking back, surprisingly lovely and exotic.) It's time to head for the carriage to the church.

At the same time (I learn later), Cecil Spring-Rice puts on his best frock coat and heads over to Brown's Hotel to collect Theodore. Because of the fog, they have to get an early start for the church. They're driving along, then Springy suddenly stops the cab, races into a haberdasher's shop, and returns with a pair of bright orange gloves for the groom. Springy tells me later, "I *had* to buy them because there was so much fog. I want Edith to know she's marrying the right man—the one with the orange gloves."

Gloves or no gloves … yes, I *know* I'm marrying the right man. For me.

Then we arrive: St. George's Anglican Church in Hanover Square. It has a very Roman look, with a pediment and five massive pillars in front. Amid swirling white fog, we enter the church.

Before I know it, the processional begins. The music sounds uncertain, a bit quavery and far away. Even the interior of this vast edifice is muffled in fog. So surreal … and I think of the oppressive, brownish-gray fog that nearly choked the city of New York the night that Alice died. This is a different kind of fog—very white and almost transparent, it gently moves, even above the altar, promising nothing bad, only good things to come.

The ceremony, conducted by Canon Charles E. Camidge, is over before I know it. Brief and sincere, soft-voiced due to the muffling effects of the fog, concluded all too soon, and then suddenly Canon Camidge smiles at both of us, saying, "I now pronounce you man and wife" and to Theodore, "You may kiss your bride."

And he does.

I finally begin to believe this is all real.

At the church Registry Office afterward, with Springy and Emily as witnesses, the new Mr. and Mrs. Theodore Roosevelt II sign the church register. I scribble my signature where indicated and then see they also require I write in my age and profession. Hastily, I write in "25" and "spinster, no profession." I look on as T writes age "28" and "widower, ranchman" to describe his status.

Widower no more.

You shan't have him, Alice. He's mine now.

The wedding "breakfast" (actually, more of a fancy lunch) is surprisingly superb. I didn't think I'd be able to eat a thing. But I can, and do, and it tastes *marvelous.* I savor each delicious bite.

Again, I tell everyone, "I'm going to quickly jot a few impressions about the wedding in my journal—no more than fifteen minutes, I promise!"

"We'll give you ten minutes only—and you've still got to change into your going-away gown!" Em is no-nonsense as she reminds me. *"Hurry!* You can't miss your train!"

We'll start our honeymoon in Dover tonight, where we'll stay for a couple of days along the White Cliffs. Then it's across the English Channel for us on the "boat train" to Paris, Lyons, and Marseilles. Eleven days later, we'll reach the balmy Mediterranean town of Hyeres in Provence, the south of France. How we'll adore strolling under stately palms, alongside red and white rose hedges, and wandering at will amid the olive orchards and orange groves—a whole new world all to ourselves.

We'll stop for several days near La Spezia in Italy to make sure that Mamma, Em, and Mame settled in at the Pensione Mauritzio.

Over and over, I remind Mamma, Em, and Mame—all of them—to "be *sure* to pack my woman's journal in my hand satchel or either of two carpetbags." (Our other luggage was shipped on ahead.)

My next journal entry will be as a married woman—married in every way, spiritually, mentally, legally, and physically.

After tonight, I will be a mysterious new stranger—Edie Roosevelt—taking my first steps into the rest of my life.

6 August 1948

Sixty-two years later and on my birthday, too.

That's how long it's taken me to write my first woman's journal entry as "Mrs. Theodore Roosevelt II."

Sixty-two years.

I still can't believe I'm finally holding this long-lost book in my hands.

(Whose are these gnarled, old hands with ghastly wrinkled skin? Surely they cannot be mine.) Nobody remembered to pack my journal properly so I could write in it during our honeymoon. (Not even me … so rushed was I in the flurry and excitement of the day.)

Somebody—there's no one left to tell me who—must have hurriedly, mistakenly, packed the journal into the wrong bag or trunk at the last minute. Then it was lost for sixty-two years.

It was my precious daughter, Ethel, who finally found my woman's journal in an old storage crate with souvenirs from our summer in London. Bless her heart, Ethel is such a comfort to me now, as a daughter should be. She always has been—which the second Alice assuredly has not.

Only Ethel and Archie are left to me now, and Alice junior.

Everyone else has "gone on ahead."

My penmanship is spider-webby and shaky now; it looks uncertain, slanted diagonally on the page.

Mamma enjoyed Italy for ten years before she died, almost as much as she enjoyed her occasional trips back to see us in America.

Mame also returned to America—and stayed there … as nursemaid to my own children … our own children, dear Theodore's and mine. What a noisy yet superlative brood they were—and some still are.

First came smiling Ted Jr., then handsome Kermit, and next dear Ethel, then little Archie, and finally our precious Quentin. (Alice was there, too—oh, no, I'm not forgetting the second Alice. As if I ever could.)

All of them were so full of spice and vinegar, laughter and troubles, so full of life!

We couldn't help having children right away— we wanted to. We craved them. We craved each other in most every way, especially physically.

Exactly nine months and eleven days after our wedding, Ted Jr. was born, looking like a little gnome. (I was so relieved when he finally grew into his body and got that one bad eye fixed. He married the loving, capable Eleanor Butler—she was definitely the making of him.)

When Ted Jr. was a young man, we were often at cross-purposes, he and I. He tried so hard to please his father ... to walk in Theodore's gigantic, immutable footsteps. I think it drove the poor boy crazy sometimes. Finally, our Ted Jr. got his heart's desire ... posthumously. The Congressional Medal of Honor for conspicuous bravery as a Brigadier General at the D-Day landing, leading his men onto Utah Beach—the only General to lead his troops onto the beaches at Normandy.

I hope he knows, somehow, and is glad. After so many years of trying so hard, amid the Teapot Dome scandal (thank God Ted Jr. and Archie were both found innocent of the charges against them) and so many other disappointments, Ted Jr. finally gave up his poor, overtaxed body on 12 July 1944, dying of a heart attack just one month after the invasion, at the age of 57. He's been gone from me several years now.

Dear, hopeless Kermit ... so sickly as a child, yet terribly good-looking, intellectual, and close to me in so many ways—at least until adolescence ... growing to be strong and adventurous, traveling with Theodore to Africa and South America's River of Doubt, where he saved his father's life. He went on two long expeditions of exploration with brother Ted in Asia. We were so happy when he married dear Belle Willard and had four handsome children. Although he was strong and active in World War I, he grew sad and washed-up by the time of World War II from severe melancholia and acute alcoholism, so much like his Uncle Elliott. Eventually, our darling son put a bullet through his brain while serving with the military in Alaska. The alcoholism finally destroyed him. I lost my beloved Kermit in June 1943.

Speaking of our golden boy, Elliott—never was there a person so doomed to experience misery, pain, madness, self-loathing, and alcoholism in his life like our dear, hopeless Nell. The older he grew, the more keenly he wished for death, for obliteration. His death was so shocking and tragic, especially because he was still so young. Even his estranged Anna, the beauty, died suddenly and young, leaving behind their ugly-duckling daughter, Eleanor, who went on to become the greatest first lady there ever was—or ever will be. Life can be surprising at times.

I thank God for Ethel, my perfect daughter in every way. Today, our neighbors still call her

"The Queen of Oyster Bay!" So she is, bless her heart. She's so much like her Aunt Bamie, right down to her chubby waistline and sharp-but-always-kind wit. (No hump on her back like Bamie, though—thank goodness.) These days, it's Ethel who keeps the family up and running. She's so efficient, hard-working, nurturing, and energetic—an ideal wife to Dr. Dick Derby. Many folks are still surprised to learn that Ethel was the first in our family to see service in the Great War—even before our four boys— where she served as a nurse in France at the American Ambulance Hospital. Her husband was there as a field surgeon. Yet Ethel has not had an easy life. She, too, lives with constant heartbreak at the loss of their only son, eight-year-old Dick Derby Jr., of septicemia. She still has her three girls, of course, but still, the pain never goes away. I know; my love—and pain— is ever-present, too. I pray God that Ethel will outlive me, even as Archie has (so far). It's a terrible, terrible thing for a mother to outlive her children.

Archie, bless his soul, is still here, generally doing things the hard way. He always did and still does. Of all our children, he's been the least bright, finding the road to learning hard. He has an outstanding war record, though, in both Great Wars. Because of his shattered knee, he's the only man to be considered one hundred percent disabled in both World War I and World War II. Recently, though, he's become so—how shall I say it?—so controversial, pro-White, and anti-socialist. Now in my eighties—with ninety not far away—I don't understand such matters and don't get into it with him. (Of course, I was never a very political person to begin with, which makes it ironic that I was once first lady of all this land.) Thank goodness for Grace, always a fine, loyal wife to Archie and the five children—two boys and three girls, and one of them another Edith. I'm glad they've always lived close by in Cold Spring Harbor, just down the road from Oyster Bay.

Quentin, my darling youngest son, was lost to Theodore and me at the tender age of twenty-one. So long ago now, it all seems like a dream. But the pain has never left me and never will. A "pursuit" pilot in the 95th Aero Squadron, darling "Quenty-Quee" was the most like Theodore out of all the boys, with so many of his positive qualities and none of his challenging ones. Quenty was always chief of "the White House gang" of young boys. He always received high marks, and he had such intellectual prowess, showing great promise as a writer while at Harvard. He and Flora Whitney were engaged, right there at the last. If only they could have married … and Quentin's line continued. He had one confirmed kill of a German aircraft in July 1918. Four days later, in a massive aerial engagement at the Second Battle of the Marne, he was shot down behind German lines and then shot twice in the head at close range.

Oh, Quenty—always so happy, hearty, and wonderfully down to earth in everything he said or did. They told us that Quentin was "one of the most popular fellows in the group." Even the pilots in his own flight would beg him to conserve himself and not have such a lack of caution. After his grave came under Allied control, thousands of American soldiers visited it to pay their respects. Oh, Quenty, your death was an unfathomable personal loss to me … and to your father, of course, who understood quite well that he'd encouraged his son's entry into the war. He never recovered from your death, and within six months he, himself, died. I made sure that a fountain was erected in Quenty's honor in France, one where village folk could come to fill up water pitchers. Sister Em was his godmother. It is still so unreal to me that my baby has been gone for thirty years.

I can't write any more about Quentin, or I won't be able to breathe. So … on to Alice. Mrs. Alice Roosevelt Longworth—known in her infancy as Baby Lee and later as "Alice Blue Gown" after the popular song in her honor, the baby girl whose delivery hastened her own mother's untimely death.

What shall I say about Alice?

It exhausts me even to think of her.

Suffice it to say, for years, we struggled together as stepmother and stepdaughter, and frankly, I was relieved when we could finally wash our hands of her dubious hijinks … handing her off into the care of her new husband, Congressman Nick Longworth.

Alice still swears to me, to this very day, that I told her shortly after the wedding: "I'm glad to see you go. You've never been anything but trouble to me."

If that's true, I certainly have no memory of it.

Alice soon became American royalty, internationally known, followed by adoring crowds, and feared for her acid tongue and behind-the-scenes power—but she has never been truly happy since the day she was born.

Alice's scandalous behavior brought her—or anyone else—little happiness. "Notorious Nick" philandered more each year, worsening with time. Alice soon realized that two could play that game and took a lover herself, eventually giving birth to Paulina, love child of Senator William Borah of Idaho.

Poor Paulina was born on Valentine's Day— wouldn't you just know it … ever the fateful day in the fateful month of February for anyone with a drop of Roosevelt blood in them. Nick died when Paulina was very young, so she only had Alice to look after her. What a sad excuse for a mother—why, a cat's a better mother than Alice is … poor child. She continues to struggle with depression and melancholia. I wonder what will ever become of her?

Alice has a famous embroidered pillow on her living room couch, which reads, "If you can't say something good about someone, sit right here by me."

But even Alice is old now. Like it or not, we're both mellowing—a little. We check in with one another if we're feeling particularly agreeable. Alice still rules in the thicket of Republican national politics—the one and only queen bee, surrounded by endless drones. Lately, she's taken up with a rising Republican youngster named Richard Nixon. Alice shows every evidence of outliving us all, even as I outlived my own little sister, Em, who died just before this last war began.

Oh Em! I really miss you (a poignant surprise to me). Such a quiet, fusty life you led in Italy, caring for Schatzi, playing canasta with other pensioners, and working in the garden. I left Schatzi with Em; I couldn't take a dog—even a dearly beloved dog!—on a three-month honeymoon through Europe.

Em, I'm so glad you became a nurse in the Spanish Civil War, dangerous as it was. At last, you found true calling and purpose in your life. You once said you wanted to be buried in your nurse's uniform. And so you were. What of dear Bamie? (Or "Auntie Bye," as the children started calling her as they grew older, due to her unflagging energy: "Hi, Auntie Bamie! Bye, Auntie Bamie!") She surprised us all by finally marrying—yes, marrying, even with her hunchback—U.S. Navy Lt. Commander (later Rear Admiral) William Sheffield Cowles. In her forties, she even bore a son, William Sheffield Jr., "Sheff," a fine, bright boy if there ever was one.

For decades, Bamie remained a close confidant of my beloved husband, her only surviving brother. She even kept a house in Washington, DC, for the longest time—18th and I Street, I think it was? Or maybe 17th?

Bamie was about seventy-five when she left us. Dear Lord, that's nearly twenty years ago, now. Incredible, yet all too true. Then there's Conie—or, I should say Corinne because she stopped going by her childhood name after Stewie fell to his death out of that college dorm window. Dear Conie … my oldest and longest friend. Although we had a few years of "falling out"—a silly misunderstanding about tickets— eventually we resumed our friendship after the deaths: Stewart, Quentin, Elliott, her husband Doug, Kermit and Theodore.

Bless their hearts … how those Roosevelt sisters both loved jumping into political debates! They were good at it, too—no flies on Bamie or Conie. Then, both sisters were always far more political than I ever was, especially Conie, more with each passing year. (But just consider the unlikely candidate who ended up as first lady of the nation: me. Indeed, truth is always stranger than fiction. I'm living proof of that.) Of Conie's four children, only daughter Corinney still survives.

Conie's later years were full of eye surgeries— one after another—and also many volumes of poetry that she wrote, published, and which sold well for a time.

I asked her once, not long before she died: "Are you ever truly happy these days?"

I wasn't at all surprised at her answer: "No."

"I'm not happy these days, either," I answered her. "Not ever. Yes, I travel the world, visit our children and grandchildren, still go to the theater and the orchestra, do what I like. But … happy? No. Actually, I feel like I'm dead."

(Yes, I actually said this to her.)

So I was quick to add, "But no one else but you must ever know, Conie. Remember how dear Greatheart used to say, 'live for the living?' I can remember waking up truly happy only twice since my beloved passed. Both times, he came to me vividly in a dream."

Before Em died, I wrote to her, "There is always pain beneath my laughter."

Yes, there is.

All right ... I can't put it off any longer.

I've been writing in this woman's journal, paragraph by paragraph, person by person ... but that one name ... the one who lives always in my heart ... that name I must now write down.

I must call up his reality, once more, upon these pages.

I know I'll be joining him soon. I hope that I will...

How can I ever describe our amazing life together? I cannot. It's all too much. It was too unlikely, large, grand, and crowded with life. It's like what Walt Whitman once wrote: "Stuffed with the stuff that is coarse and stuffed with the stuff that is fine."

It all passed so quickly, again, like a dream.

Like Lincoln, my darling has "belonged to the ages" now for lo, these twenty-nine long years.

I have lived alone, without him, for twenty-nine years.

Every day alone, I think back over our days, months, and years together as he moved from step to step: Federal Civil Service Commissioner ... Police Commissioner and President of the New York City Police Board ... then on to Assistant Secretary of the Navy ... the role of beloved Colonel of the Rough Riders (when I used to sleep alone, with his letters to me pressed against my heart) ... next, Governor of New York ... then Vice President under the doomed McKinley ... and finally President of the United States, with me as First Lady—not just once, but twice.

Such a meteoric rise some would say is divinely guided or ordained, and I, for one, believe it.

Theodore once told me: "In much earlier days, I used to walk by the White House sometimes, and my heart would beat a little faster as the thought came to me that possibly ... possibly ... I might someday occupy it as president." He did, bless his heart, and, for the most part, gloriously.

Even Bram Stoker, famous author of the book Dracula, once told me before the troubles in

Cuba: "This guy has got to become president someday—a man you can't cajole, frighten, or buy."

He was so right.

I was happy in the White House—so happy that I felt I should throw a ring into the sea or something to show my thanks to the universe. Our White House days were the first time in ages when we didn't have to worry about money! Most of Theodore's family money was spent on those blasted Dakota cattle, nearly all of which died in a horribly gruesome manner during the hard winter of 1887–88. Everybody's cattle pretty much died then. The great cattle ranching bubble finally burst.

Throughout our marriage, Theodore was only too glad to relinquish to me the purse strings—and the entire family purse. I loved tightening up our budget and cutting out heaps of unnecessary expenses, getting us on a more balanced footing.

During our White House years—every single day—we'd spend a private hour together from 8 a.m. to 9 a.m.—just us two, nobody else, not even the children (Mame and the maids took care of that, fortunately). Usually we took a private walk around the grounds together. Other times, we'd go horseback riding in Rock Creek Park. I worked on endless first lady duties. Every day, I'd personally read and clip four different newspapers for my husband to keep us both up with current events. I worked very hard, so hard that I hired the first social secretary for the first lady, ever—dear, good Belle Hagner, what a gem she was! I helped design the revamping and enlarging and then personally did all of the redecorating of the White House—taxpayers had to agree to spend the money because we had far too many children and nowhere to put them.

I created the lower level painting gallery of "First Ladies in the White House"—my own idea and a good one. I created the Colonial Gardens, containing heirloom flowers that Martha Washington and Dolley Madison once planted. When I saw the odds and ends of crockery at the White House, I immediately ordered thirteen hundred and twenty pieces of plain white Wedgewood dishes to spiffy up the place. In all things, I tried my hardest to make the White House a place of great music, books, culture, and art. I continuously advised my beloved husband whenever necessary. (Actually, a lot.) He always used to remind me, "Whenever I go against your judgment, I always regret it later."

Our larger-than-life existence wasn't always good, of course. I think of that time when Theodore was shot at close range by a disgruntled madman. I can never forget the two miscarriages (August 1888 and May 1902)— one a boy and the other, a girl—children who we would never know in this lifetime.

It feels so good to write in a woman's journal again … reams and reams of writing … I've missed it so! But my brain is no longer nimble, and I'm happy to have Mrs. Jessica Kraft helping me with paperwork these days. Mrs. King, at our local library, also remains my close friend and assistant.

Last month—when I was hit by another spate of racing heart spells—I told them both, individually (and also told Mary and Bridget, my maids), "I'm probably going soon, but I have no regrets. It's been a full life." I also reminded them, "When I am dead, please don't let them take off my wedding ring—and please, no embalming."

Also, I want my epitaph to read: "Everything she did was for the happiness of others." (There are some who might disagree, but I don't care. I tried the best I knew how, and that's got to count for something.) "I only want the simplest of coffins, covered with my favorite shawl. I'd like some pink and blue flowers from my children and grandchildren ... those who remain after I'm gone."

Whatever else, don't take off that wedding ring.

Oh, Theodore, when are you coming to fetch me home?

It was that damned River of Doubt in the Amazon that hastened your death, I just know it—the recurring malaria, constant infections, pustules—ghastly things to endure. But what's done was done—nothing to change that now.

As Theodore lived his last day, he told me he felt very odd. "Almost as if my heart is about to stop."

Instantly, I telephoned for Dr. Briggs, who arrived quickly, checked Theodore all over, and said, "Nothing looks to be wrong. It's just your imagination, sir."

Did Theodore tell me that he loved me on that last day?

Not exactly ... but to me, what he said was even more meaningful—and it was just like him to say it. He told me, "I wonder if you really know how much I've truly loved our lives together, here at Sagamore Hill?"

With tears springing to my eyes, I answered, "I do know, darling, I do. I've loved it, too."

The doctor and I also promptly fetched James Amos, Theodore's beloved black valet from his White House days—who we all loved dearly—to help me care for him. (Fortunately, James was able to catch an afternoon train from the city.)

Theodore continued to feel uncomfortable and "odd" for the rest of the day. The doctor gave him an injection of morphine to help him sleep. Dr. Briggs suggested I sleep in the adjoining bedroom—Ethel's old room—while James tended to Theodore, should he awaken and need the privy. James slept (lightly) on a daybed, set up in a corner of the room.

I never thought I'd sleep that night. But I must have fallen into a fitful doze because I was startled by James' light rap at my door around 2 a.m.

"Ma'am ... the Colonel does not seem to be breathing, ma'am." (He always called his master Colonel Roosevelt, never Mr. President.)

I remember that I couldn't feel my bare feet on the floor as I rushed into the bedroom I'd always shared with my husband—except for tonight.

James turned on the electric bedside lamp.

Theodore looked perfectly serene, as if sleeping. His face seemed a bit dusky. There was no sound of any breathing whatsoever.

I stroked his cheek and the hair above his forehead. "Theodore, darling..." I spoke, hoping against hope. His forehead was already cool. I knew. It was 6 January 1919.

Now Theodore, too, had become one who "belongs to the ages."

"Thank you, James. Would you leave us, please? I want to be alone with my husband."

"Yes, ma'am. I'm so sorry, ma'am," James replied as he left the room.

I turned off the electric light as James closed the door.

In the darkness, I climbed upon the bed and lay down beside my late husband. I tucked in beside his inert body in its white nightshirt. Embracing him with my left arm thrown across his chest, my right hand holding his left, I pressed my nose and lips against the side of his neck and breathed in his scent, one last time.

I must have stayed like that for an hour or more.

I did not cry, but I couldn't stop trembling, violently.

I whispered to him, first mentally, then aloud, words of love and farewell, wishing him safe passage to wherever the journey took him next.

Finally, I knew it was time to let the world know...

I pulled on a robe, hanging from a hook behind the door, and shut the bedroom door behind me—for the last time, it turned out. I tiptoed downstairs to inform the servants, who were no doubt awake and starting their morning work in the kitchen.

I was dry eyed (yet still quivering), an automaton as I told them of their master's passing. Oh, such a caterwauling rose up from them as has never been heard on Earth before or since!

I still couldn't cry, not until that second night, when I opened the door to our bedroom. He wasn't there, of course. The undertakers had taken him away.

I quickly closed the master bedroom door and moved next door to Ethel's childhood bedroom. I cried.

And cried some more, until I willed myself into oblivion.

Never again would I occupy the double bed that Theodore and I shared together. Just like Martha Washington, who could never again bear to enter the room where she'd been so happy with George.

Was Theodore a perfect husband? No. But he was perfect for me, despite the long absences between us when wanderlust got the better of him, and out he'd go to the American west, Africa, or Cuba.

Was he a perfect father? Not really, and it bothered me terribly sometimes. Although he loved the children dearly—his "bunnies" as he called them—he was overly strict with the boys.

He "bent the boys' twigs" as he thought they should go, never acknowledging that he endured such things in his own youth that he forced—by love—for them to do now.

Ted Jr. was pushed far too hard by his father. He felt he never measured up to his illustrious sire. In his early teens, young Ted came close to having a nervous breakdown. He so dearly wanted to attend Annapolis or West Point to become a military officer, but Theodore told him no, he must first attend Groton and then go on to Harvard, as proper young men of his class have always done. For many years, Ted was miserable, until finally … finally … he came into his own much later in life.

Poor, dear Archie—our boy who was never the quick-witted scholar—wanted desperately to accompany the Great White Fleet around the world in 1907–1908. The admiral even sent him a personal invitation. But Theodore said, "No, you too must go to Groton and then on to

Harvard. In this family, it is expected of you."
No Great White Fleet for Archie.

All of our boys hated Groton and detested Headmaster Peabody. Yet all of them attended there, against their desires, to please their father. Theodore himself never went there because he was still too asthmatic and frail in body to be away from home.

Kermit ... ah, he was once secretly my favorite child—so handsome and thoughtful, intelligent and literate, adventurous and brave. He even saved his father's life along the River of Doubt. But he inherited too much of his Uncle Elliott's— and my father's—love for alcohol. Groton and Harvard didn't do him much good in the end.

Dearest Quentin ... the son who was the most like his father, brilliant, cheerful, natural, unspoiled, clever, good with his hands, clever with his brain and wit, and deeply kind. He, too, went on to Groton and Harvard, uncomplainingly.

In the Great War—I still call it that, despite its new name, World War I—our four boys had no choice about going into the Service, long before any draft. It was simply a given. Theodore was chomping at the bit to meet the challenges, privations, and adventures that warfare promised, and his sons—ready or not— faced these challenges on their father's behalf because the latter was now too old and sick to face them himself.)

Quentin gave his life for the cause, and neither Theodore nor I ever got over it.

Was I the perfect soulmate for Theodore, even as he was for me?

The simple answer to that is … no.

Was Alice Hathaway Lee his perfect soulmate, as so many postulated?

My emphatic answer to that is … not even close.

Then, who?

The answer always was … and ever shall be … Fanny Smith, Frances Theodora Smith Dana Parsons—my old friend from school, who worshipped Theodore, utterly and without question, for the rest of her life.

She always loved him and approved of everything he did—and I do mean everything. Be it his lackadaisical attitude toward money (luckily, I saved and invested our money, paid the bills, and managed our properties); his weakness for wearing fanciful uniforms and rose-colored satin waistcoats (I gently but firmly "disallowed" these fancies, especially in public); or his propensity to bite off more than he could chew concerning feats of derring-do and life-or-death challenges out in the wild. Fanny always urged him on with glowing eyes and a flashing smile. I quietly begged him to temper his adventures with a dollop of caution. I did not want our children to live without their father, nor I without my beloved husband, no matter how many mountains he ached to climb or broncos to ride.)

I must say, never did adversity break Fanny's spirit, despite so many tragedies of her own: a miscarriage during her first marriage to Navy Commander Will Dana (who she married only because Theodore was already engaged to Alice) or Will's untimely death in the first flu epidemic of 1890. Six years later, she married James Russell Parsons (after Theodore unexpectedly married me). He was a politician in New York State and later a diplomat in Mexico City (thanks to Theodore's influence). They had a son, Russell, and a daughter, Dorothea, who died as a toddler. James was killed in a collision of a trolley car with his carriage. Then, Fanny and her little boy were alone in the world. She used to hold up Theodore as an example to her son as the sort of man he should be.

Fanny went on to become a best-selling author of How to Know the Wild Flowers and the author of four more (very popular) nature books. Following James's death, she moved back to New York City, where she became an active supporter of the progressive arm of the Republican Party. (Unlike myself.)

Ah, Fanny. She might have made Theodore initially jolly and would have been glad to have T be a naturalist for his career, living in happy obscurity and near-poverty, with adoring Fanny cheering him on all the time, no matter what he did or didn't do, or what he forgot to do.

But it was I who always loved him and took care of the details (so many tasks, large and small) to spare him the burdens of real life so that he could readily co-create with me a happy marriage, so he could rise to national prominence of which I never dreamed, to become an agent for good to so many people nationwide.

In the long run, I believe Alice Lee would have been too shallow and spoiled to succeed on this life journey with him. Fanny, always too indulgent of Theodore's often wild ideas, would have been unwilling to keep him more "tethered to the Earth," something required to make any marriage—or national politics—work. Fanny attended Theodore's funeral at the Oyster Bay church.

But I could not.

I remained at home, with the blinds drawn and the door shut. I did not want to break down in public. Private person that I am, I could only do so while alone.

Fanny is still alive and kicking, as they say, somewhere in New York City. I thank God on bended knee that she never did catch Theodore between wives.

MANY DAYS LATER:

Bridget just brought up my dinner on a tray. I told her I'd nibble a few bites and then put my own self to bed. I won't be needing her tonight. I want to be alone with my thoughts.

As she exits the room, Bridget reminds me, "Remember, ma'am, I'll be waking you early before the carpenters arrive at nine to nail down the new floor boards." She's referring to a few half-completed repairs to the floor in the northeast corner of my bedroom at Sagamore Hill. A couple of the maple floor boards have started to sag a bit when I totter across them.

Late yesterday, two workers showed up in my bedroom to remove the offending wood and replace it with new planking. They weren't able to complete the job yesterday because their work ran later than expected, so they're coming tomorrow morning to finish installing the two planks and start applying matching stain and varnish.

Last year, after a particularly bad heart spell, I burned all of my personal letters between Theodore and myself—boxes and boxes of them … oh, so many. It made my heart ache, but I didn't want our private marriage bed to become fodder for gossip columnists. That's what Martha Washington did with the letters between her and her beloved old man, as she often called her George.

If it worked for Martha, it would suffice for Theodore and me, too, so I burned our correspondence.

But this journal … this beloved, long-lost woman's journal that only just came back into my hands today—I just can't do it.

I can't burn it. I can't destroy this story of us.

I must be able to hide it someplace, where no one will find it for years and years … until no one will be interested in Theodore and me anymore.

But where?

Under the floor, of course.

The answer comes to me from beyond myself. Could it be…?

I place my pen between my teeth and proceed.

With some difficulty, I pull a pillow off my bed, drop it onto the hardwood floor where the opening is, and then tuck my journal under one arm while I kneel upon the pillow (with faint groan of pain that I try to keep inaudible) so I can peer into the vacant space between the joists beneath the floor. (I hope I'll be able to get up again without calling for Bridget.)

There's plenty of spare room between the pieces of lumber—a miniature, dusty highway between the first and second floor. Perfect. I'll place my journal there and push it far out of the workmen's sight with my right foot—my strongest.

I flop from my knees over to one side so that I'm now sitting on the floor, awkwardly sideways on my right hip.

I've written this long last diary entry (I'm almost done), but I better make this fast. Someone might come to check on me and see me writing in this dear old journal—these words that I'm writing right now … that you are reading right now, whoever you may be.

Farewell (soon) to all of this … and hello (soon) to a new adventure, with Theodore. That alone will be Heaven enough for me.

In closing, I paraphrase the words of Robert Browning from his poem "Love Among the Ruins," one of our favorites. (Theodore and I actually met Robert Browning once, in England. What a thrill it was for us both, even if Browning was seventy-five and noticeably querulous at the time.)

So often, Theodore quoted this poem from memory to me, word for word … but now I change the "she" to "he."

I send this poem forth now as my telegram into the unknown realms: Come now, Theodore. Please … I'm ready.

When I do come, he will speak not,

he will stand, either hand on my shoulders,

he will give my eyes the first embrace of his face

Ere we rush,

ere we extinguish sight and speech,

each on each.

Edith Kermit Carow Roosevelt

6 August 1861–30 September 1948

The End

Acknowledgements

W hen I was about 10 years old, I watched a "live" television drama about the great love triangle of young Theodore Roosevelt, Edie Carow—his childhood sweetheart—and the glamorous heiress Alice Lee.

The story grabbed my imagination then and never let it go. Once the plot stewed in my head for several decades, I decided to write my own vision—my own *version*—of the romantic Roosevelt love story, a tale of tragedy and triumph.

To help sharpen my memory, I turned to the incredible, prodigious *Roosevelt Trilogy* by Edmund Morris—*The Rise of Theodore Roosevelt* (Book 1), *Theodore Rex* (Book 2), *Colonel Roosevelt* (Book 3)—a literal treasure trove of information.

Edmund Morris' wife, Sylvia Jukes Morris, also wrote her own Roosevelt biography, entitled *Edith Kermit Roosevelt: Portrait of a First Lady.* Louis L. Gould's *Edith Kermit Roosevelt: Creating the Modern First Lady* was also a valuable resource.

I would also like to thank the multi-talented, marvelous crew over at Paper Raven Books, without whom this tale would never see the light of day. Like author Betty Smith wrote in the preface to the second edition of her best-selling tale *A Tree Grows in Brooklyn:* "Thanks so much, you guys! Thanks a whole bunch!!"

With thanks and gratitude,
Jane Susann MacCarter

Check out this adventure/time travel/ romance novel by Jane Susann MacCarter: *Twice Upon A Kiss*

You get to choose *one* life this time around—and only one.

Which will it be?

• Life in the Present Day where you're unattractive and awkward but still manage to connect with an overweight, nerdy boyfriend who is lukewarm at best. It's no great love match, but hey, at least it's something. And it *could* lead to more—but at least you know it's *real* and happening now...(or is it?)

...or...do you choose...

• Life in Jarmo—a 7500 BCE Neolithic paradise in what's now the Middle East. In Jarmo, you're a strong, beautiful woman with a gorgeous, god-like man by your side who is deeply in love with you. You're doing a world of good for your primitive tribe. Only...part of you senses that this life might *not* be real...(or is it?)

What if your Jarmo life is really just a fever dream brought on by brain trauma inflicted on you during your twenty-first century existence?

Which life is the real life? Both? Neither?

Your choice. Pick one.

And *only* one.